THE
PLUTO
X C U I V X Z W D W E X H J W
PROJECT
▲

3 4 7 2 5 2 9 1 4 5 7 4 3 6 1

MELISSA GLENN HABER

DUTTON CHILDREN'S BOOKS

DUTTON CHILDREN'S BOOKS
A member of Penguin Group USA Inc.

Published by the Penguin Group
Penguin Group (USA) Inc., 375 Hudson Street, New York, New York 10014, U.S.A. • Penguin Group
(Canada), 90 Eglinton Avenue East, Suite 700, Toronto, Ontario, Canada M4P 2Y3 (a division of Pearson
Penguin Canada Inc.) • Penguin Books Ltd, 80 Strand, London WC2R 0RL, England • Penguin Ireland,
25 St Stephen's Green, Dublin 2, Ireland (a division of Penguin Books Ltd) • Penguin Group (Australia),
250 Camberwell Road, Camberwell, Victoria 3124, Australia (a division of Pearson Australia Group Pty
Ltd) • Penguin Books India Pvt Ltd, 11 Community Centre, Panchsheel Park, New Delhi - 110 017,
India • Penguin Group (NZ), Cnr Airborne and Rosedale Roads, Albany, Auckland 1310, New Zealand
(a division of Pearson New Zealand Ltd) • Penguin Books (South Africa) (Pty) Ltd, 24 Sturdee Avenue,
Rosebank, Johannesburg 2196, South Africa • Penguin Books Ltd, Registered Offices: 80 Strand,
London WC2R 0RL, England

ACKNOWLEDGMENT
The poem "From the Dark Tower" (p. 57) is from Copper Sun, copyright 1927 by Countee Cullen,
published by Harper, New York, New York. Rights are held by the Amistad Research Center at
Tulane University, New Orleans, Louisiana.

CIP Data is available.

Published in the United States by Dutton Books,
a member of Penguin Group (USA) Inc.
345 Hudson Street, New York, New York 10014
www.penguin.com/youngreaders

Designed by Jason Henry
Printed in USA • First Edition
ISBN: 0-525-47721-7
1 3 5 7 9 10 8 6 4 2

■　■　■

THIS ONE PRETTY MUCH HAS TO BE FOR

SECRET AGENT DANIEL J. SPIRO.

THE
PLUTO | PROJECT

THEY HAD BEEN WAITING in the culvert for over forty minutes. Finally, Juliet flipped over onto her back. She rubbed her sore elbows and sat up.

"They're not coming."

"Sure they're coming," said Alan hurriedly. "We just have to be more patient."

"They didn't come yesterday and they're not coming today. I have to go home and practice."

"Aw, come on, Jules! Just a little longer."

She hesitated. "All right," she groaned. "For *you*." She lay down again, but even out of the corner of his eye, Alan could see he had lost her attention. She was doing little foot exercises; she was not really with him anymore.

He tried something else.

"So, are you going next Friday?"

"Next Friday?"

"You know—to the dance."

"To the *dance*?" she hooted. "Do I seem that lame?"

"Well, you dance, don't you?" he defended himself. "It could be fun."

"Sure, I *dance*, but not with *those* morons. Listen, how much longer do I have to stay? I really have to practice. I only did twenty minutes this morning because we had this stupid brunch thing with some friends of my mother's."

"Ten minutes. I promise. Ten minutes and then I'll let you go. And you don't have to practice so much, do you, if you're so good?"

"*Yes*, I have to practice if I'm so good. And I'm probably so good *because* I practice. And besides, I *want* to practice. But you wouldn't understand that."

Alan rolled over. The frost on the ground crackled under his weight. "I can't imagine wanting to do the same thing over and over, like that," he mused, idly watching the clouds that drifted lazily across the sky. "I can't imagine anything that I'd like to do that much."

She sighed elaborately. "We've already been over this— it's because you don't have a calling. That's what dance is for me, a calling—it's something I *have* to do. I couldn't *not* do it. But you're not like that. Like today—if I go home, you won't stay and see if they show up. You'll go home instead."

Alan shrugged. "It's just more fun when you're here, that's all."

"But what about Fordham? Don't you need to stay here and protect her? Or are you going to admit it's just a game?"

"It's not a game!" said Alan hotly. But then she hushed

him, laying her hand over his mouth. Silently, she pointed up to the road that ran overhead.

The white Ford Probe was back. It parked just off the bridge, and a man came out on the driver's side and waited, smoking a cigarette. A few moments later footsteps came crunching up the road—just like they'd been waiting for.

The whole thing had all started off as a joke. Of course it still was a joke, but not the way it had been when they'd first started the game, back on the first day of eighth grade. The first day was a half day, an enormous waste of time—they might as well have had another full day of staring at the walls at home, rather than having to stare at the pockmarked dropped ceiling of Josiah Quincy Junior High. It wasn't like they *did* anything in that waste-of-time half day anyway—just a lot of filling out of forms and the passing out of textbooks and reminders to *please*-cover-the-books and *please*-respect-school-property and *please*-don't-lose-them-or-you-will-be-charged that they heard every year.

Alan sat with Alice and Agnes, just like he always did. Of course he got some crap for sitting with the girls, but that was to be expected, the way you have to expect to get pimples every now and then. It used to drive Alan crazy, the sheer irrationality of being called a fag for liking the company of females, but he had learned pretty quickly not to try and reason with the nimrods that populate a junior high school. The best strategy, he had discovered, was to lie low and be *unobtrusive.*

Unobtrusive—that was the word Mrs. Perry had used to describe him, back when he'd first had her for sixth-grade English. He used to sit in the back of the room, doodling on the edge of his notebook, his feet on the back of Alice's chair in front of him. He never raised his hand, even though he always knew the answer, but if he ever started any trouble, Mrs. Perry would fix him with her steely gaze and say, "I see you back there being *unobtrusive,* Mr. Green." Old Mrs. Perry. He really liked her.

Now he had her for English again. Secretly, he hoped she'd asked for him, pleaded with the principal to let her teach eighth-grade English so she'd have the honor of teaching Alan Green once more. Of course, if she had handpicked her class, she wasn't as smart as he'd thought she was, because she'd let in Keith Reese, too, and next to Alice, Keith was Alan's closest friend. Time had proved again and again that they were not above getting in trouble when combined together—you just had to ask Alan's Aunt Trish.

Now Alan sent Keith a conspiratorial grin, and that was how he saw Juliet for the first time. Usually Keith's mountainous bulk would have blocked the view, but this new girl was so majestically tall that Alan could easily see her proud head right over Keith's lumpy frame. She was totally different from the other bland and mealy students in the class: long and lean, with an interesting mass of coiled braids on the back of her swanlike neck. When

Perry called on her, she looked up confidently and gave her name as Juliet Jones. Juliet Jones: a gorgeous name, and she looked gorgeous, saying it. *Juliet Jones. I just moved here from Ithaca, New York.*

She stuck out a mile in that sea of white faces, not only because of her dark skin but because she was a head taller than anyone else: five foot ten in stocking feet, six foot four *en pointe*. That was what she said after class, when everyone asked how tall she was. "Barefoot, or *en pointe*?" she'd asked, and when no one knew what *en pointe* meant, she'd shrugged, rolled up onto the toes of her sneakers, and walked down the hall away from their staring eyes.

She was beautiful; at least Alan thought she was beautiful. He liked her skin, her incredible smooth reddish-brown skin, and he liked the mysterious mess of black and shiny braids that sat on the back of her neck. But above everything else he liked the serious intensity that shimmered around her: *Juliet Jones. I just moved here from Ithaca, New York.*

Alan Green, he introduced himself to her in his head. *I've been living in this suburban wasteland all my life.*

When his last class let out, Alan shoved his way down through the clogged stairs as quickly as he could while still retaining his aura of nonchalance. He was not completely honest with himself about his motives, but he did let himself look for her ramrod straightness out of the corner of his eye. She wasn't anywhere, but there were the others, waiting for him by his locker, just like they always did, just like they always would.

"What a like effin' waste of time this day is," Jethro was saying as Alan came up. "What's the plan now?"

Alan shrugged as he glanced down the hall. "I was kind of thinking I'd ask that new girl from English if she wanted to come and hang out with us," he said.

"What new girl?" asked Alice, surprised. "And since when do *you* go out of your way to be nice to the new kids?"

"Why not?" he protested. "It's an act of kindness, a *matzvah*. That's what my grandmother would say."

"Jesus, Alan, I'm not even Jewish and I know it's a *mitzvah*. And since when are *you* practicing random acts of kindness?"

They all laughed. It *was* kind of funny, when you thought about it. Alan was more the type to practice random acts of irony. He had no interest in being *nice*. Instead he preferred the words Mrs. Perry had used to use to describe him: *curmudgeon, cynic, misanthrope*—a person who doesn't really like other people.

"Misanthrope," he'd repeated, back when she'd first called him that in sixth grade. "Misanthrope. I like that."

"I didn't mean it as a compliment," she'd commented wryly, but he knew she had. He might be young in years, but already he knew it was irrefutably less cool to be *nice* than to be a cynical misanthrope.

Now he turned to the others. "I'm turning over a new leaf," he confessed. "And I can't very well be the welcoming committee if you're all here looking over my shoulder. Run along, little children. I'll meet you at the big rock."

They grumbled, but he knew they would wait for him. What else could they do? He was the glue that held them together, the motor that made them go. And if they teased him about Juliet later, who cared? As he had so often explained to Keith, the secret to being truly cool was not to care what anyone thought, not even your closest friends. In fact, he theorized, perhaps the main purpose of having friends was to use them for not-caring practice. With them, you perfected the impassive face you showed to the rest of the world.

Now, standing in front of the long row of lockers, Alan practiced looking impassive, *detached, nonchalant*. It was, to say the least, a challenge to maintain his cool detachment while standing there like a dope in the empty hall. Alan shifted his weight from foot to foot. He felt uncomfortably exposed there, standing alone against the row of ugly orange lockers. Even with his *unobtrusive* face on he felt like a single zebra standing on the veldt, just asking to be eaten. And then, just as he thought it, there came one of the lions sauntering up the hall.

Rory Frankel's fists were lightly clenched as he came, and his head bobbed up and down as if he heard the cheers of thousands saluting him. Alan stiffened instinctively as Frankel approached, but then, just as he had practiced during his frequent confrontations with his father, he forced himself to go loose: loose and uninterested and totally cool—*sang-froid*, just like Mrs. Perry had said: cold blood.

"Yo, Green," Rory grunted as he came up to Alan: this

is what passed for conversation among the Frankel brotherhood. He socked Alan fraternally (and painfully) on the shoulder and then continued ahead, listening to the invisible multitudes shouting and clapping and hoping to hell he wouldn't clobber them, too.

Alan was still standing there, rubbing his sore shoulder, when, miraculously, Juliet came striding down the hall like an advancing whirlwind. Alan smiled. It was a miracle of miracles, a sign—her locker was right near his, only eight lockers away. She stood there, jiggling the lock and jerking the door up and down as she tried to open it, and this gave Alan the chance to be chivalrous. The lockers were terrible; they always stuck. You saw a lot of sixth graders carrying their crap around all day because they couldn't get those stupid lockers open.

"Hey," he said when he'd released her possessions from their confinement, "I saw you in English, didn't I? Julia? Is that right?"

"Juliet," she said. "Like the play."

"Alan Green," he answered. "Like the color. So hey, my friends and I were going to go and hang out this afternoon . . . do you want to come?"

Juliet Jones arched an expressive eyebrow at him. "What do you mean, *hang out?*"

Suddenly Alan felt unexpectedly awkward. He had planned out all sorts of cool repartee with this Juliet Jones, and now she was playing with his head. "I don't know," he stammered. "Play video games . . . talk . . . *you* know. . . ."

"I don't play video games."

"Well, board games, then. Sometimes we play board games."

"I don't play board games, either."

"Cards?"

"I don't play any kinds of games."

"Jesus, Juliet!" he said to her in honest disbelief. "What have you been doing with your life?"

"Dancing. I've been dancing."

"What do you mean, dancing? Like this?" He bit his lip and clenched his fists, swinging his hips with exaggerated awkwardness.

"*No,*" Juliet said, laughing. "Not like *that*. I do *ballet*."

"Ballet!" Alan repeated. "Isn't that a little"—he cast around for the right word—"square?"

Juliet snorted. "*Square?*" she repeated. "No, *this* is square." And she bit her lip, clenched her fists, and swung her hips around with exaggerated awkwardness. "Sorry, Alan Green—I gotta go. I have to practice."

"Wait—" Alan called after her. He didn't really have anything to say, but watching her walk away with no closure like that was a sock to the stomach. "Does that take a lot of time, all this ballet?"

"I practice a couple of hours a day, and I take classes three days a week. I'd take more, if I could, but it's very expensive."

"*Man,*" Alan breathed. "What do you do for fun?"

Juliet Jones stared at him.

"That *is* what I do for fun. Why else would I do it?"

"I mean—my parents used to make me take music lessons. I pretty much hated it."

"Which instrument?"

"Oh, guitar, drums, a little keyboard, you know."

"*Oh*," said Juliet, raising her eyebrows. "You're one of *those*."

"One of whats?"

"You're one of those people—you *drift*."

"Drift? I'm not even fourteen years old yet! I'm *supposed* to drift!"

Juliet shrugged. "Whatever," she said. "Have a good time hanging out. I'm going to practice."

And Alan was forced to watch her walk away, tall and proud and inexpressibly graceful. The air around her shimmered with her intensity, the way the desert gives off heat.

"Couldn't get her to come, huh?" Keith guessed when Alan joined them outside.

"Naw. She preferred to insult me in there."

"Oh, poor Alan." Alice moved over on the big rock and mock-tenderly held his head before grinding her knuckles into his scalp. That's the way it was with Alice—she gave you pretended sympathy and then a good strong dose of reality: just what the doctor ordered. It was much better than the soppy sympathy you got from useless Agnes. Now useless Agnes was sitting there with her big sad spaniel eyes, feeling sorry for him. Well, there was no need to feel sorry for him—Ballerina Juliet was no big deal, and nothing had changed. They still had five hours before any of them had to go home for dinner.

"So now what?"

"We could go across the field to my house—I think Frankel's gang is done beating up Kaufman."

"Already? Man! It's only the first day of school—you'd think they'd ease him back in—give him a half day or something."

Jethro stood up and demonstrated the way the gang had jumped on Kaufman. "They let him get like almost across the field, and then they ran at him—woof! Right in the friggin' kidneys. You'd think he'd like learn to go the long way around."

"Maybe it's a point of honor."

"Maybe it's brain damage from last year."

"He should just like stand up to those goddamn bastards. If he wasn't like such a friggin' wimp, they'd probably like leave him alone."

"Sure," agreed Alan and Keith dubiously. The five of them sat on the big rock, looking out over the field. None of them admitted to waiting for Frankel and his gang to clear the field before they crossed it, but it's a fact of life that it's easier to be *unobtrusive* when there's no one around to see you.

Alan had once mentioned to his aunt how many kids got beat up at Josiah Quincy—not on the day he'd had the fight, but a couple of weeks later. Trish had waited until they were all sitting down at the table before she'd mentioned it to Alan's father that night at dinner.

"Alan says a lot of kids are getting beat up at school, Mitch. And I heard that Myra Kaufman's thinking of sending her son to private school. She says he's getting traumatized."

"What will private school teach him?" asked Alan's father around his mouthful of food. "It just teaches him to run away from his problems. Learning to deal with this crap's probably the most important thing the kid'll get out of junior high."

Yeah, right, Alan thought. *When do you have to deal with getting beat up outside of junior high? How often do* you *have to worry about getting challenged to a fight, Dad?* But he smiled brilliantly at his father and said, "Yes, *sir.*"

His aunt caught the sarcasm and reached over to touch his face. "Are you okay, Alan? They're not giving *you* any trouble, are they?"

Alan shook his head. He wished he hadn't brought any of it up. He still felt sick to his stomach when he thought about the stupid fight he'd been in—even though it hadn't been all that big a deal. It had just been him and Richard Paas, circling each other in a big ring of stupid horse-faced kids shouting *Fight! Fight! Fight!* until he felt like screaming, *If you want to fight, come on, take my place!* But humiliation and fear had kept him silent.

Richard Paas had looked cold and clammy, too—Alan was pretty sure he hadn't wanted to fight, either. He'd probably woken up the same way Alan had that morning, sick to his stomach and wishing for anything—a sudden flu, a freak snowstorm, a meteorite smack in the middle of Josiah Quincy Junior High—anything to keep him home. But like Alan, he must have known that each day he put it off was like pumping air into a balloon over his head with the word COWARD shimmering on it. And Alan was pretty sure you could not remain *unobtrusive* with a big balloon that read COWARD hovering over your head. So he'd gone to school and watched the hands of the clocks turn with their spasmodic jerks through each sixty minutes, bringing him successively closer to the inevitable moment he was supposed to meet Richard Paas on the blacktop. It was all so stupid! In theory, there were important things to fight about in the world, but Alan had been pretty sure then and was pretty sure now that whatever had brought him out to face Richard Paas on the blacktop wasn't one of them, not even close.

He hadn't even been able to explain to Alice what the fight was about. All he knew was that it had been his turn.

"What do you mean, it was your turn? What did you do?"

"I have no idea."

"You must have done something!"

"Yeah—breathed. And been born with a penis. That's it, I swear! Frankel's stupid pimply goons just tapped me, and said it was my turn."

"Well, tell Kellerman or someone. Get one of the teachers to break it up."

"Then they'll just pound me on the way home." He was very weary. If truth be told, he *was* a coward. He didn't like fighting, and he certainly didn't like pain. Pretty much the only time he'd punched anything was when he'd punched the punch clock that time they'd visited the potato chip factory. He'd done it to make Alice laugh, but he'd done it harder than he'd meant to, and it actually hurt his hand a little. But relatively speaking, the clock had been an easy opponent. And now he was supposed to wait for Richard Paas on the blacktop and circle around him until one of the teachers came to break it up, and somehow that would prove his mettle.

So Agnes had bribed Louis D'Angelo with a week's lunch money, and Louis D'Angelo had gone to get the guidance counselor, and Kellerman had come barreling down the hill to the blacktop with his tie over his shoulder and his brown suit flapping all around him, bellowing like a bull, and that had been that: Alan's first fistfight. *Yeah, Dad. Real essential education.*

Now Alan remembered that conversation as he sat on the big rock and watched Kaufman stagger off the field. Poor Kaufman. It was probably too late for him. There's not much you can do to get out of the crosshairs once you've already been marked: each black eye was like the bull's eye of a target. And if that wasn't fair, well, Alan was enough of a cynic to know that life isn't fair. That might not be a life philosophy, but it sure as hell fit his experience.

There was always this problem of where to go on Wednesday afternoons. Alice and Agnes's house was pretty good, because they had a really big TV and a whole closet full of old board games, but their mother was paranoid about having boys in the house and chaperoned them all too closely. Keith's house was fine, but it was all the way on the other side of town, and by the time they all got their bikes and made it there, the afternoon would be gone. Jethro lived nearby, but he always came up with all sorts of excuses why they couldn't go to his house. Alan knew it was because he was embarrassed—embarrassed because his house was small and kind of squalid and his mother was kind of squalid, too. There was always crap all over the place, and the house had kind of a funny smell. It wasn't so bad—you got used to it pretty quickly—but Jethro always looked so pained and twitchy whenever you were at his house that it ruined any fun.

So it was pretty obvious they should hang out at Alan's. His house was close, it had no funny smell (unless you thought Lysol was funny, which you might), and there was no nervous mother there to try and chaperone you. It was also gigantic. That's what everyone said when they came over: "Man! Your house is so *big!*" It really was. It was also strangely empty, because the furniture from the old, smaller house had to be spread out through the seventeen rooms and five bathrooms and the greenhouse off the dining room. The empty rooms gave the house a weird abandoned look, but Alan's father always said he worked too hard to have time to buy any furniture, and Aunt Trish said it was a job for a wife, not a sister, to spend his money. Alan didn't care. It made his father seem eccentric, not just rich, to have that enormous house sit empty all the time.

So Alan's house was perfect, but they couldn't go there on Wednesdays because the maid was there that day and he wasn't allowed back in until five. This seemed stupid to Alan—they could just hang out in his bedroom while the maid cleaned the rest of the house and in his other room when she cleaned his bedroom, but though he was perfectly willing to piss off his father, his friends weren't. So now it was 1:10 on a Wednesday afternoon, and they still didn't know what to do.

"Tell them," Agnes told Alice shyly.

"Tell them what?"

"*You* know—about the game."

"That stupid game . . . ?" Agnes turned away from her sister, blushing, but by then they all wanted to know. Finally, Alice explained. There was a concrete culvert that ran under the road behind the police station, built for a river that had long since been diverted elsewhere. Alice and Agnes had gone there one day and listened in to what went on up above. It was a popular spot, that road, and you could catch little fragments of conversation as people walked over it. And this was the game: there was a list of things people might say, and if you heard them say them, you got to eat a bite of doughnut. Here was the sort of things they had on the list:

(From anyone on a skateboard) *Hey man, check me out:* one bite.

Nice weather, huh? Or any variation: one bite.

Any swear worse than *damn* or *hell* or *crap:* two bites.

"You're right, man," Keith yawned to Alice, "that *is* totally lame."

But something about the game appealed to Alan, so they went. They crossed the field and made their way to the town center, where they bought a dozen doughnuts. Then one by one, with all the secrecy of rampaging rhinoceroses, they dashed from their hiding places down the little embankment to hide in the culvert.

It's a funny thing, but when you eat doughnuts very slowly, you get pretty giddy. Before the last bit of jelly had squirted down Agnes's shirt, they were all laughing so hard that someone came out of the police station to check the report that some kids were smoking pot in the culvert. And that was the beginning of the game that ended up not being a game.

▼

WHEN THEY'D BEEN PLAYING the game every day after school for about a week, Alan was suddenly struck with the force of inspiration.

Alice had brought along a clipboard. She'd written out the top ten things they'd overheard from the culvert, and they'd decided they couldn't go home until they'd checked them all off. But it was too easy: they'd gotten them all in twenty minutes.

"You'd think with ten thousand words at people's disposal, they'd use more of them," complained Keith. "Do you think they *know* how boring they are?"

It was at that moment that the fire of genius fell upon Alan. "Oh, they know," he told the others, speaking in the hushed tone of prophecy. "They *know*. They're speaking in code."

"Of *course*," breathed Alice. "Why didn't we see it before?"

"I don't get it," said Jethro sullenly. "Whaddya mean, they're speaking in code?"

"It's very simple," Alice said, proving yet again why she was Alan's best friend. "There's a group of spies—"

"Conspirators," put in Alan.

"A group of conspirators, and they're planning a—"

"Assassination."

"An assassination, and they have to talk in code."

"Yeah," said Alan, warming under the fire of his genius, "like this—here, chuck me the clipboard, Ag—uh, *How's it goin'?* means—I don't know . . . 'What's the status report?' And *Hey man, check me out* means 'I've completed my mission.' And when someone says 'I love you,' it means they've picked another victim. Like that." He paused for effect. "It's a conspiracy, I tell you, and the only thing that stands between it and the destruction of the free world is the five of us." He laid down the pencil and sat back, triumphant.

"A conspiracy," echoed Alice in a somber voice. "Do you think it's . . ."

"It is," Keith intoned. He put on his lowest voice: "I'm afraid we're looking at the work of . . . *Conspiracy Rule American People.*" It took them a minute to work out this acronym. Then they all cracked up, except uptight Agnes.

There's hardly anything more fun than being spies. Alan had had some experience on this front, back two summers before, when he and Alice had invented their brilliant spy organization, the SRU, and its intrepid leader, Roberta Bismo.

Alan had discovered Roberta in the supermarket. When you live in a benighted little suburb, as they did, the supermarket is sometimes the only place to play on a rainy day. They had been walking up and down the aisles, looking for clues for the SRU to interpret, when a package of Pepto-Bismol had fallen off the shelves next to Alan's feet. It was clear what it was: the Pepto-Bismol phone. Alan answered it, holding it to his ear.

"It's Roberta Bismo," he whispered to the others. "Our intrepid leader has instructions for us."

"Who?" Alice asked.

"Roberta Bismo—she's calling us on the Pepto-Bismo phone."

"It's not Pepto-Bismo," Alice corrected, "it's Pepto-Bismol, you schmuck."

"Oh," Alan said. "I thought it was Pepto-Bismo." It didn't matter. On whatever phone it was, Roberta was waiting for Alan to relay her instructions. That first day, the instructions were mostly to find other phones: the pineapple phone, the Cheerios phone, and finally the Tampax phone, which call uptight Agnes refused to take. Alice tried to get Alan back for that one, and when it was her turn, she sent him to find the Preparation H phone. Agnes was too embarrassed to go anywhere near the hemorrhoid cream and drifted off somewhere else, but Alan marched over, picked up the box, and smiled wickedly at Alice. "Guess what?" he asked her. "Roberta wants me to tell you you're a pain in the ass." Ah, the SRU. It was the most fun they'd ever had.

"What ever happened to the SRU?" he asked Alice now. "An organization like that, it should have gone on forever."

Alice and Agnes exchanged uncomfortable looks. "Your mother died," Alice said finally.

"Oh, yeah," he said. "Right. That."

It might have been awkward then, except that a car rolled by overhead and stopped unexpectedly.

Later Alan included that moment in the company of the great historical coincidences—like the Pilgrims suddenly coming upon a Wampanoag who spoke English on the shores of Cape Cod. How miraculous it must have seemed to them, standing on that foreign shore in their funny hats and their buckled shoes, when a man who must have appeared to them as a savage stepped out of the woods and addressed them with a chipper "Welcome, Englishmen! Do you have any beer?" This moment was like that: a coincidence of epic proportions. Not ten minutes after the SRU had uncovered the existence of Conspiracy Rule American People, two members of that dread organization came to rendezvous just above them.

Now the leader of the SRU put his finger to his lips and signaled for them all to be quiet. Silently, they turned their ten ears upwards. They heard the creak of the car door and a grunt as the driver hauled himself out of his seat; ten ears took in the footsteps that crunched through the gravel. There was a crumpling sound and the faint sigh of a match being struck. Then ten eyes flew to the south:

more footsteps were coming to the middle of the bridge above them, scraping footsteps that belonged to someone too lazy or too gimpy to pick his feet fully off the ground. A skateboard clattered by. When all was silent above, the man who was smoking coughed and spoke. Ash from his cigarette fluttered down from above them.

"How's it going?" Ten eyes flew down to the clipboard where Alan had written *How's it goin'?*—"What's the status report?" Eight eyes flew up to Alan's. He shrugged, silently, modestly. Ten eyes flew back up to the ceiling of the culvert, as if their collective gaze could bore right through the concrete to reveal the members of Conspiracy Rule American People standing above.

The second man began to speak: it was all they could do to keep from laughing. His voice was too villain perfect, the perfect Henchman voice. Alan looked at Keith; his lieutenant was about to lose it. Alan drew his finger across his neck.

"Poifect," the Henchman answered, and every one of the five of them heard the unsaid *Boss.*

"I love it when you tell me that," the Boss said, and the cigarette came flying down into the dry streambed like a falling flame. Then he got back into his car and drove away. The Henchman scuffled through the gravel, and then he too was gone. When all was silent above, Alice and Keith exploded.

"Did you *hear* that? He said it: 'love.' Just like on the paper. Alan, you're a *genius*. How did you know which phrases were part of the code?"

"Brilliance," explained Alan modestly.

"Wait a minute," Jethro objected. "He didn't say, 'I love you.' He said, 'I love it when you tell me that.'"

"Oh, come on, Jethro!" Alice reproved. "Spies can change their code a little to make it sound more natural. You *know* we've discovered something." She turned to Alan and her eyes sparkled. "I think the SRU has been resurrected, Agent 666. And if I'm not mistaken, that's the pinecone phone ringing for you right now."

He picked it up. "Yes, Roberta," he said into the pinecone. "Yes, we're on them both—the Boss *and* the Henchman." He waited, and then dropped the pinecone into the gutter. "Secret Agent 55378008," he intoned, the long number tripping off his tongue with the ease of practice, "our services are needed again. Roberta requests that we take up our posts here tomorrow."

They started walking back up the embankment, when Alice suddenly called out, "Hey . . . look at this." She was holding up a small piece of metal in her hand. It might have once been part of a broken key ring, but to the trained spies of the SRU, the piece of metal was ominous.

"A C," said Keith.

"A veritable C," echoed Alan.

"So it's true," said Keith. "They've left their sign. Conspiracy Rule American People is afoot."

"CRAP," Alan confirmed. "CRAP indeed."

Wednesday was quickly shaping up to be the worst day of the week. As always, it started badly, with Aunt Trish coming in and nagging him to clean his rooms because the maid was coming. As always, Alan objected that it was ridiculous to have to clean up for a maid, but Trish said Mary was paid to dust and vacuum, not to pick up Alan's dirty underwear. This morning she'd gotten more annoyed than usual and called him an ungrateful snot.

"Trish called me an ungrateful snot," Alan complained to his father when he entered the kitchen.

"I didn't say you *were* an ungrateful snot," Aunt Trish clarified as she followed him to the table. "I said that if *I* had complained the way *you* complain about someone cleaning my room for me, *my* parents would have told *me* I was an ungrateful snot."

This was in fact what she had actually said, but to Alan it was a distinction without a difference. In point of fact, he *was* an ungrateful little snot, but he didn't feel too bad about it.

After breakfast, Wednesdays never got better. It was gym day, which was always painful—it was hard to be *unobtrusive* when Coach Pinhead Nonecksky was encouraging some smelly hulk to lob a ball at your head. Wednesday lunch was also something of a disaster. This year Alan had been stuck with the ridiculous Wednesday lunchtime of 10:50—a time when civilized people take breaks for tea and crumpets instead of Tater Tots and sloppy joes. The uncivilized hour was made infinitely worse because no one else was stuck with it—no one Alan knew at all, except Morris Kaufman.

Alan was no idiot; he knew that part of being *unobtrusive* was not to associate yourself too closely with notable victims like Kaufman. Ever since preschool, Kaufman had been a marked man. It was a mystery how he'd managed to perfect that look of miserable vulnerability at such a young age. If Kaufman had been a zebra, he would have been picked out of the herd by the mangiest of lions—no, not just the lions. Any self-respecting carnivore on the veldt would have gone after him and taken him down. Hell, even the other zebras would have turned on him and started tearing at him with their flat zebra teeth—how could they not? Long before the bullies of Josiah Quincy Junior High had singled Kaufman out for tenderizing, he had shuffled nervously through his day, his pointy Adam's apple bobbing constantly in his throat, his thin wrists twitching, speaking only to reveal the most exquisite expressions of dorkiness. Even Alan wanted to hit him, sometimes.

Now Kaufman raised his miserable eyes to Alan, pathetically begging him to sit down. Alan ignored both look and looker. He did not believe in cooties, but he did believe in loser germs, and he did not want Kaufman's loser cooties on him.

And there, two tables beyond Kaufman, was a tall and glorious excuse: Ballerina Juliet. How had he missed that she shared this Early Lunch of Losers with him? He gave quick thanks of praise to the Loser Lunch Gods before going to stand beside her.

"Hey," he said, "can I sit down? You'd be saving me from a fate worse than death if you let me sit with you."

She raised an eyebrow at him.

"Alan Green," he said, motioning to himself. "I talked to you on the first day. You're in my English."

"Right," she said. "The drifter. Sure—sit down. What fate am I saving you from?"

"Kaufman," Alan said, opening five packages of ketchup over his Tater Tots.

"Kaufman?"

"Kaufman." He jerked his head in Kaufman's general direction. "The skinny kid over there. No, don't look—are you crazy? A look is like a lifeline to a loser like Kaufman. You don't want to give him that opportunity—he's like a leech. Besides, you don't want Rory Frankel's gang to think you're fair game, too. I've already had to fight them once, and I don't want to do it again." He said this with more bravado than he meant, as if the fight had been more than circling around Richard Paas and throwing a few mock punches as they waited for Kellerman to break it up. But even as he thought about it, his stomach tightened with the stupidness of it all.

"Rory Frankel's gang?"

"You know, that big black-haired kid with the fart of goons that follows two steps behind him?"

"A *fart* of goons?" she repeated.

"You know—like a gaggle of geese. A murder of crows.

A business of flies. Anyway. They've been after Kaufman ever since sixth grade."

Juliet looked shocked. "Why doesn't anyone do anything about it?"

"What's anyone going to do? It's not like Kaufman can walk around in a bubble all the time. It's not like anyone's going to arrest a junior high school bully anyway, especially when his dad is a cop." He winced: now he sounded like his stupid father.

Juliet was looking indignant. "Maybe he just needs better friends," she said.

"What, are *you* going to be his friend?" Alan asked, spork halfway to his mouth. "Don't do it. It's death, *death!* I tell you. And you don't want Rory Frankel and the Frankelettes to notice you."

Juliet gave him a condescending look. "You think they *haven't* noticed me? I don't exactly *blend in.*" This was true: he had never noticed how short and white his school was before. "I've already been introduced to Rory Frankel's gang, I think."

"Is someone bothering you?" Involuntarily, his fist clenched, as if he were leaping to defend her honor. Then he winced. Too *Godfather*—he sounded like an idiot.

"Those shrimps?" she sniffed. "They don't scare me. They *disgust* me."

Alan considered this; they disgusted him, too, but mostly they made him scared. He shook his head as if to clear his thoughts and tried again. "Hey, what are you doing after school? My friends and I . . ." He was just try-

ing to figure out how to explain the SRU, how to down-
play the obvious geeky aspects to the game and highlight
the fun and brilliance of turning random comments into
the stuff of spies, but Juliet didn't even let him finish.

"I'm going to see the doctor about my foot."

"What's wrong with your foot?"

"Hurts. It's okay—it always hurts."

"What can you do about it?"

"Hurt the other foot, so I don't notice this one."

"Huh," said Alan, and then he launched forward again.
"Well, what about tomorrow?"

"I have dance class tomorrow," she said. "Every Tuesday,
every Thursday, every Saturday."

"Don't you ever skip?"

"Not unless I'm barfing. Otherwise I go, even if I'm
hurt. Last spring, I was out with a stress fracture for *two
months*, sitting in the back and just having to watch."

"Oh," he said inadequately. And then: "Are you that
good?"

"*That* good? How good do you mean?"

"Good enough that this isn't just a hobby."

She fixed him with her big brown serious eyes until he
almost squirmed. "I *want* to be," she said. "And if I'm
going to be, I don't have a lot of time for board games or
whatever it is that you and your friends do when you hang
out." Alan must have stiffened then, for she softened her
tone. "That was bitchy—I'm sorry. I'm not like that,
really—I'm just tired of explaining it. Really, thanks for
inviting me." She picked up her tray then and carried it

across the lunchroom, indifferent to the eyes that fell upon her. With infinite grace and beauty, she tipped the remains of her hamburger and Tater Tots into the overflowing garbage pail, and then she floated out of the lunchroom.

■ ⊞ ■

That afternoon the members of the SRU returned to the culvert. Alan had written up another list of encoded terms the nefarious CRAP might use in their bid to take over the world: *nice weather* and *got a light* and *have a good one* were all there, along with several dozen others. Agnes didn't want to go. She had a test.

"We all have that test," Alan pointed out. "Come on, Secret Agent 000, which is more important, a stupid Spanish test, or keeping America safe for democracy?"

Agnes gave Alan a stricken look with her big spaniel eyes. It was amazing how that go-ahead-and-hit-me expression made her look so different from Alice. Once, at a sleepover, he'd woken himself up at midnight to see them asleep, to see if with eyes closed and mouths unmoving he could trick himself into not being able to tell them apart. But even in sleep there was no confusing Agnes with Alice. She slept more fitfully, more awkwardly; she breathed through her mouth and her face twitched in her dreams, while Alice slept on, cool and collected, all her secrets held deep within her, locked in little boxes, fastened with triple locks.

"Come on, Ag," he told her now. "Roberta's counting on us."

Agnes looked back and forth at them, her miserable eyes swelling with tears. At last, Alice couldn't stand it. "All right," she sighed. "Sorry, Alan. We'll be back tomorrow." Alan watched them clamber back up the embankment. They had always laughed at how Alice and Agnes had to do everything together, but Alan secretly thought it might be nice to have someone you wanted to be with that much.

Once he'd asked Alice what she was going to do about Agnes when she got married, and Alice had gotten all uncomfortable and shrugged.

"Maybe I won't get married," she'd said. "Maybe Agnes and I will just come to live with you, in your enormous house."

"But what if *I* get married?" he'd asked her, out of curiosity.

"I don't know," she'd answered. "Maybe you and I should get married—you know, to keep each of us from marrying anyone else."

"All right," he'd agreed, shaking her hand.

Now she was calling down to him from the top of the embankment. "Secret Agent 666!"

"Yeah?"

"Call us if they come, all right?"

It was not five minutes later that a car came crunching up the road. It stopped just where the white Ford Probe had parked the day before, and once more the door creaked open. Heavy footsteps moved to the edge of the bridge. In a minute, the smell of a cigarette floated towards them on the September breeze.

"I'm going to reconnoiter," Alan mouthed, pointing up the embankment. Keith shook his head, squaring his brows and waving his hands as if to say *abort, abort*. But Secret Agent Alan Green 666 began slithering up the hill on his belly, reckless of danger, his fingers digging into the dry dirt for leverage as he crawled, commando style, towards his prey. There were the wheels of the car, now, caked with mud, though it had not rained in days. A muffler badly in need of repair. And a license plate—a vanity plate—CPR 1.

Alan slithered back down to the blind where the other spies were waiting. Jethro looked at him quizzically, but Alan put his finger to his lips. From above them, the sounds of the Henchman's footsteps were coming, undeniably the same as the day before: one foot dragging while the other stepped firmly.

"When's it supposed to rain?"

"I hear tomorrow."

"Excellent. Well, give my regards to your wife."

"Yeah, my wife." And they both laughed. It was just like the day before—the cigarette came flying down in a flaming arc, and the Boss climbed heavily back into his car.

The three of them let out a collective breath as the Henchman shuffled away. Then Alan scuttled over and grabbed the cigarette butt.

"Look at this," he said, holding it out to the others.

"What is it?" Jethro asked, turning it over in his hands and neatly obliterating any fingerprints.

Keith understood. "There's no mark or anything—no filter," he said.

"That's right," said Alan. "I heard in World War One soldiers smoked their cigarettes backwards so no one could recognize what army they were in by the mark on their cigarettes. That's what this guy did. He ripped off the filter and smoked the marks on it away." A pleasant thrill came over him as he spoke. "That's not all," he said. "I got the license plate. CPR 1."

"CPR? Like, what is he, an effin' lifeguard?"

"*No*, Agent Idiot, he couldn't get CRP—it's too close to a swear. They won't let you do it, like they wouldn't let my cousin get SHTBOX. CPR—you get it? He's just as good as admitted that he's the leader of CRAP."

The others stared at him in admiration: Alan's logic was unassailable.

"This is unbelievable," said Keith finally. "I mean, what are the chances that *we* would have stumbled on this vast international conspiracy?"

"If *we* hadn't, then this story would have been about someone else," reasoned Alan. "Come on, it's only coincidental from our point of view. *Some*one was bound to discover them—they're not exactly being discreet."

"So what now?" Jethro ventured. "How do we like figure out what they're trying to do?"

"We consolidate our notes." This is what they had mostly done in the SRU, filing reports in triplicate with the help of an old typewriter and reams of carbon paper from the Dumpster behind Ace Stationers. Now they took

Alan's allowance and bought a new file folder. With great solemnity, they opened a new case.

"Well," Keith drawled when they were done, "if I were CRAP, I'd certainly watch my back now."

Alan scowled at him, a little. Games like the SRU are really the most fun when you pretend you really believe them.

Thursday was overcast and unpleasant, the kind of fall day that reminds you that winter is coming. As they sat in the cramped, chilly culvert, Alan and Alice conferred about the suspicious conversation, interpreting every nuance and keeping ears pricked for the sound of the Boss's car. But no car came. The electric excitement of the day before was gone. Alan kept on trying to excite the troops about the conspiracy, but it was very hard. Finally, he gave up.

"Hey—you know that girl, Juliet?" he asked suddenly.

"Which Juliet?"

"The new girl. The tall girl."

"The black girl?"

"Yeah, her."

"What about her?"

"Do you know she practices ballet like ten hours a week?"

Keith snorted. "Well, *that's* a waste of time," he said.

Alan was suddenly offended. He felt very protective of

Juliet and her obsession. He imagined what she was doing at that moment, pliés and revelés and whateverés in a tutu and those blocky pink toe shoes he'd seen in her bag. He didn't like Keith saying it was a waste of time. Then he thought about Keith prancing around in a tutu, and the idea was so funny he laughed out loud.

"What?" asked Alice, poking him with a stick.

"Keith in a tutu." That was all he needed to say to crack them all up.

Obligingly, Keith lumbered to his feet and began miming putting on a leotard. He hauled on invisible straps too tight and jumped a few times in the air as he tried to stretch them farther. Then, lips pursed, delicately and daintily, he tried to stretch the seat of the leotard over each cheek of his enormous ass: all this while gracefully holding the gauzy skirt of the tutu over one arm. Alice was nearly in tears from laughing; Alan, close to asphyxiation, wondered in a panic if he would ever stop laughing long enough to draw in a proper breath. Keith was an amazing actor. He could mimic anything—his specialty was mimicking bad mimes. That was what he had, instead of being *unobtrusive*. You could see how the other kids looked at him, thinking he was just a big lard-ass, sloppy and awkward and always spilling over the sides of his chair—and then he would start to mime something. He was so spectacularly talented that it allowed him a protective measure of cool.

Alice looked at her watch. The road above the culvert was mostly empty. A few skateboarders rattled overhead without saying anything for the SRU to interpret. Even Alan was beginning to feel bored when Alice stood up and brushed the dust off her jeans. "I'm going home," she announced.

"I should go home, too," chimed in Jethro. "I've got like a crapload of homework to do." Alan rolled his eyes. Jethro was always swearing with this fierce, bad-boy expression on his face, but he never used a real swear, even if you offered to pay him—Alan had tried. It was always *frig* this and *crap* that and the serious bad-boy look as if he were some sort of hardened gangster. Alan wasn't ever sad to see him go, but this desertion challenged his leadership. He took the situation in hand.

"We shouldn't have expected them today," he said to his spies. "The Henchman told the Boss it was going to rain *tomorrow*—that means *today's* the day they put their plan into action. We'll have to wait until tomorrow to hear what they did."

"You're full of crap," Keith yawned. "No matter what happens, you'll say that it fits in with the conspiracy. They're here, it means something, they're not here, it means something. . . ."

"What can I say?" Alan shrugged. "As Sherlock Holmes said, sometimes it's the dog that *doesn't* bark that makes all the difference." Then, before anyone could undermine his authority by leaving, he led them out of the culvert and up the embankment towards the center of town. Within seconds of returning to civilization, it seemed, they heard the news that the governor had been shot.

A LAN WAS SITTING IN HOMEROOM, reading *The Catcher in the Rye* under his desk, when Ms. Sanchez announced that they would be having an assembly at nine that morning.

"Why?" Alan asked, looking up from his book. In the seat beside him, Nancy Friedman looked visibly shocked.

"For the *governor*," she said. "Didn't you *hear*? Didn't you wonder why all the flags were at half-mast?"

Alan hadn't noticed the flags; he wasn't all that patriotic.

"Did you know about this?" he asked Keith now. "Is that why your fly's at half-mast?" They both cracked up, sending out little sideways looks to see who else was listening. Nancy Friedman sniffed with disapproval. Alan stopped laughing and looked at her curiously.

"Why are *you* so cut up about it?" he asked. "Did you know the governor?"

"Of *course* I didn't know her," Nancy said primly. "And if you don't understand why it's a *tragedy*, well then, I think you're less than human." She applied herself very diligently to listening to Ms. Sanchez take attendance, as if to show Alan what an inhuman lout he was.

Alan shrugged. All that morning, and all through the assembly, he still couldn't feel anything at all for dead Governor Murphy. He didn't really understand why they should have an assembly for her when they'd never had one before for anyone else who'd died—not even for that janitor who'd been found dead in the custodian's closet. People were always dying; you couldn't take too much notice of it or you'd spend all your time in assemblies with Kellerman scowling at you from the stage when you didn't look sad enough. And if you really wanted to take notice of death, why should you ever raise the flags to full mast again? Governor Murphy was going to be dead forever, after all. Maybe the flags should have to stay at half-mast until someone else died, and then they could be lowered to quarter-mast, and then to eighth-mast, and so on, until you had to dig a hole ten thousand miles down to lower the flag into, because death was piled up on all sides.

But really, he couldn't feel anything for dead old Governor Murphy, and he was restless as the teachers tried to help the children handle their supposed grief and confusion. He wasn't grieving, and he wasn't confused. The only emotion he felt was the pretend conviction that the SRU had uncovered the assassination before it happened and an eagerness to go out and look for more clues with his spies.

"It's pretty strange, isn't it?" he said to Alice, for the fourteenth time, when he saw her and Agnes in the halls.

"I mean, it's pretty amazing that we were expecting something like this."

"We weren't expecting something like *this*," she corrected. "In the game *I* was playing, I just thought they were going to knock over a bank or something."

"You thought CRAP was going to knock over a bank?"

"*No,*" she said, smacking him on the arm. "I don't think there really *is* a CRAP, you dope."

"But maybe there really *is*," Alan argued. "I mean, it's a pretty freaky coincidence that we predicted it."

Agnes hugged her books to her skimpy chest and sniffed. "I don't think you should be so happy about it," she said. "The governor's really dead, you know."

"I know," he said defensively, but he didn't really care.

He was still unmoved in English class, where Mrs. Perry wanted to process the governor's death even more. And because he knew Mrs. Perry liked him, for all that he was *unobtrusive* and *misanthropic* and *cynical*, he felt that frankness was in order.

"What if we don't actually care at all?" he asked bluntly. "I don't exactly get why we should care about this so much."

The look of pity and consternation that Mrs. Perry shot him was not what he had expected: it almost made him wish he'd said nothing at all. But then again, the secret to cool was not to care what anyone else thought. He made his face impassive again.

Mrs. Perry was pacing up and down in front of the blackboard. Her blouse was untucked on one side, and it made her look all disheveled. Alan wished she would do something about it, but Mrs. Perry apparently had other things on her mind.

"There are at least three reasons you should care," she was saying. She looked at Alan solemnly before she included the rest of the class in her gaze. "The first is that politics cannot be separated from politicians. Without Fiona Murphy in the State House, many of the programs she championed will languish and die. And those programs affect *you*—she has worked long and hard to get art and music back in the public schools, for example."

She paused for a moment as if waiting for Alan to care. He had to be honest: he still didn't. Mrs. Perry started again.

"And two, even if you disagree with her political agenda, you cannot disagree that a democracy cannot flourish under the threat of violence." She paused again, staring out the window where the flag snapped at half-mast in the slanting rain. "I lived in the sixties," she said in a strangled voice they had never heard from her before. "You cannot imagine what it was like, to see great leaders picked off, one by one, by cowards who knew that they would lose at the ballot box. Assassination . . ." She choked up then, and they had to wait for a moment before she went on. "Assassination of a democratically elected leader is worse than murder," she declared. "It is the murder of democracy itself."

Her eyes were actually filled with tears. The students squirmed uncomfortably at their desks. Alan felt the blush rising in his cheeks for her.

"There is one last reason. . . ." She reached into her desk and pulled out a dog-eared book. "Listen, class," she said. "I'm going off-road, off-lesson plan today." She strode up to the blackboard and wrote out something in her beautiful handwriting, while they stared at her, astonished.

"A long time ago," she said when she was done, "a long time ago, when anyone in a parish died, it was the tradition to ring out the church bells nine times to tell of the passing, and then the bell would ring out the years of the dead man's life. And people might rush to the church, when they heard the bell toll, to find out who had died. And John Donne, a great poet, lying in bed ill, wrote this as he heard the bell ring. 'Now, this bell tolling softly for another, says to me, Thou must die.' And this is what he wrote, meditating on that thought." She pulled away from the board so they could see what was written there, and in a cracking voice, she read it aloud:

"No man is an island, entire of itself; every man is a piece of the continent, a part of the main; if a clod be washed away by the sea, Europe is the less, as well as if a promontory were, as well as if a manor of thy friends or of thine own were; any man's death diminishes me, because I am involved in mankind; and therefore never send to know for whom the bell tolls; it tolls for thee."

No one spoke when she was done; there didn't seem to be anything to say. But Mrs. Perry disagreed.

"All right," she said. "We have twenty minutes left in the period, and you have twenty minutes left to write to me about this poem." There were generalized groans at that, but because they all liked Mrs. Perry, and because they wanted her to stop sounding like she was going to cry, they all dutifully took out their notebooks and began writing.

In the seat in front of him, Ballerina Juliet was staring down at her empty paper, but Alan liked to write. He liked to look at the words the poet used, and he liked how easy it was for him to find meaning in the words and between the words and in the words not used. Now he wrote about how cleverly the poet tricked you into seeing his point, how he started so abstractly, choosing to focus in the beginning on the island, rather than the man ("entire of *itself*," not entire of *his* self), how the poem moved from small (the clod) to big (the promontory) and then suddenly to the personal (a manor of thy friends); how the sudden appeal to the reader (*thy* friends) awakened them to the guilt of indifference (not, this is what *I* would feel, but rather think of how *you* would feel), and then the grand idea that we are all intertwined, and the morose corollary that we are all constantly diminished by death, and that our own death is foreshadowed every time the bell tolls. It was a fine little piece of prose, classic Alan Green, who was good at English, but he didn't really believe it. Fiona Murphy might as well have been an island. Her death did not touch Alan at all.

■ ⊞ ■

The rain continued. It rained for six days straight, heavy, sodden rain the color of metal hanging like a pall over everything. School was damp and the awful smell of wet wool came out of every locker. Mrs. Perry and the other teachers were still visibly upset about the governor's death. When kids were laughing in the halls, Kellerman glared at them as if they were laughing at a funeral. But then again, Alan said to Alice, how long were they supposed to pretend they were upset?

"I mean, come on!" he said to her. "We didn't even *know* the governor. After my *mother* died, I didn't wait for a week before making jokes again—and that was my *mother*."

"*You* were making jokes at your mother's funeral," Alice reminded him. "I don't think we ought to be looking to *you* as an example."

Alan flushed. The uncensored memories of his mother's funeral were always leaping up unwanted before his eyes, and he had not yet learned how to banish them. Now he saw Alice and Agnes sitting in the temple, still and respectful in their black dresses, Agnes's so new it still had one of the price tags on it. The price tag dangled there, under her collar, and it had bugged Alan all the way through the service. He tried not to look at it. He tried to comprehend the fact that this was the last time he'd be sitting in a room with his mother. But he couldn't help think about how Aunt Elisheva had mentioned that his mother had been dressed in a suit she'd never had a chance to wear, and then, involuntarily, inappropriately, he'd wondered if they'd taken the price tag off her clothes before they sealed her into that box of lead. Then he'd just gotten giggly. It wasn't funny, not at all, and he knew it. He couldn't explain it, either, unless it was the tranquilizers they'd given him, and he just sat there in the front row of mourners and laughed and laughed until he'd cried. Then everything got all swimmy, and the next thing he knew he was back in his own bed. It was the second time he hadn't been able to say good-bye to his mother. She'd been dumped into the cold ground, ashes to ashes, dust to dust, without Alan saying good-bye. And now Fiona Murphy was there, too. Maybe the two of them would meet up in heaven for coffee and discuss what a little bastard Alan was: an ungrateful little snot and a cold-hearted SOB.

"I don't think we should be doing this anymore."

Alan looked up from the newspaper.

"What do you mean, Ag?"

"This—this *game*. It's just sick. She's dead, really *dead*, and you're acting like it's a joke!"

"We're not joking," Alan pacified her. "We're spies, remember, Secret Agent 000?" He looked down to the mutilated newspaper before them. Keith was busy scouring the paper for clues, adding up the letters of the names of anyone mentioned in the articles to see if they revealed any numerological patterns. Alice sat beside him, a Scrabble board in her hand, just in case CRAP had eschewed the usual A=1, Z=26 code for some more complicated Scrabble scoring, where J=8, Z=10, and so on. Jethro was making lists of initial letters of the article's sentences to see if they spelled out messages from one CRAP operative to another, and Alan was sitting with the unusual prop of a Bible on his lap. Every now and then he had Alice and Keith give him strings of numbers that could be translated into biblical verses. Suddenly he set the book down.

"Omigod," he said. "Look at this, look! There *was* a hidden message. Look where you led me—Judges 9:30. 'When Zebul the governor of the city heard what Gaal son of Ebed said, he was very angry.'"

The others stared at him. At last Alice summed up their reaction.

"Huh?"

"*The governor.* It says it right there, Zebul *the governor.*"

"But her name was Fiona," put in Agnes.

"I *know* her name was Fiona!" Alan snapped. "But did you hear? Zebul *the governor!*"

"That's what I'm saying!" Agnes burst out. "This is all a joke to you, but the governor is dead, D-E-A-D, *dead.* It shouldn't be a joke—it's really serious."

"Give me a break," said Alan, closing the Bible on Zebul and Gaal son of Ebed. "Before last week, you didn't even know her name, and today you're crying about her? What about all the other people who died today? Are you going to get all teary about them, too? People are always dying, Ag, like . . ." He cast about for an appropriate analogy and seized on the words Mrs. Perry had written on the board. "It's just like clods falling into the sea. You just can't think about it all the time."

"Maybe she's right," said Alice, looking up at her sister. "Maybe she's right, Alan. Maybe it's not funny."

"Maybe it's hypocritical to act like we care," Alan countered. "What about that?"

Agnes shook her head stoutly. "I just think it's wrong," she said, as if that were some kind of argument.

She kept on saying it, too, for a week, until it stopped being any fun at all. First Alice decided to agree with her sister, and then Keith said he thought the whole game was stupid anyway, and then, just around Alan's birthday, when it had begun to get really fun, the SRU slipped back into inactivity.

Fortunately, something else had come up to entertain Alan before he risked boredom. For his birthday, his father had given him a video camera. It wasn't a digital one like it should have been—his father was a cheap bastard—but it was still flat-out the best present Alan had ever been given. Alan went out right after breakfast to film, even though it was practically a hurricane outside. The wind kept blowing leaves right into the lens, and the rain kept getting in his eyes, but still, it was perfect. No one was out, and the wild wet world seemed full of strange creatures. The branches cast crazy shadows on the ground as they whipped about in the wind, and they looked to Alan like grasping hands. Alan filmed it all, and he felt ridiculously pleased with himself as he watched his little movie later on his VCR. Ballerina Juliet was wrong: he *could* have a calling; he could be a great movie director like Hitchcock or whoever else was supposed to be a great movie director. After lunch, he sat at the computer for two hours and pounded out a screenplay. He cast the usual suspects in their roles before turning his sights on potential stars. Marshaling his courage, he reached for the phone. There was only one new listing for Jones.

"Excuse me?" asked Juliet's voice, when he'd made his pitch.

"I'm going to make a movie. Alice and Agnes Parker and Keith Reese and Jethro Plante are going to be in it, and you should be, too."

"A movie." Not a question this time, just a statement of unadulterated disbelief.

"I mean, it's not a *film* or anything—just a movie. Can you come over here this afternoon?"

"Sorry," she said. "I have two dance classes on Satur-day." And she hurried him off the phone.

For a moment, Alan sat there, disappointed. But when you thought about it, it was really her loss, though the movie they began that afternoon could not truly be called a great artistic success. They had filmed it in one of the empty rooms on the third floor of Alan's house, and they all agreed it might have looked better if they'd spent as much time setting up the lights as they had making the props. And, Alan had to admit, if they'd spent as much time making the props as they had playing video games in preparation for prop making, the movie might have been better still—but all that meant was that they might still be geniuses, if they put their minds to it.

The plot centered on an eccentric old gentleman who threw a dinner party with the antisocial plan of murdering his guests. Alice was supposed to die at the dinner table. Because they thought it would look good if someone could pull her head up by her hair and have her food all stuck to her face, they spent an instructive half hour testing the adhesive properties of various foodstuffs: peanut butter, honey, whipped cream. They were so interested in affixing food to Alice's face that the actress had to return home for dinner before her scenes were shot. On the afternoons that followed, they attempted several other scenes, including a rolling-down-the-red-carpeted-staircase scene and a hanging, but none of these looked entirely convincing when they crowded around the shaky images on Alan's TV.

What they needed, Alan decided, was blood. This precipitated more hours of prop development, given that they had finished the ketchup at lunch. In the end they used a whole bottle of corn syrup, colored with food coloring and flavored with Rose's lime juice. Agnes was supposed to fill her mouth with it and spit it out in a sanguinary spray when her head was slammed (gently) in the door. This was Alan's first crisis as a director.

"Is it palatable?" he asked her solicitously. "Is it tasty?"

"*No,*" choked Agnes. She had her worried look on, her eyebrows almost disappearing under her hair. She turned to Alice for help. "I *can't* have that in my mouth—it's disgusting."

"Of *course* it's disgusting," Alice soothed. "It's *blood*."

"It's *way* more disgusting than blood. It's all thick and gross and *nasty*."

"Oh, come on, Agnes!" Alan encouraged. "Suffer for your art!"

"Alan," said Alice firmly, "we can't make her do it. It's too disgusting. She—"

But Alan had found a new tactic. "Please, Agnes," he said, "for *me* . . . ?"

Agnes looked at him miserably, spanielly, and filled her mouth with the blood. Then (all the while looking like she was going to barf) she let her head be slammed (gently) in the door.

Suddenly Alan didn't want to shoot the scene anymore.

"This is stupid," he said angrily. "She looks worse before she spews than after. Can't you do *anything* right, Ag?"

Agnes looked at him, the lime-flavored blood still dribbling out of her mouth. A big wad of hair was stuck to her cheek.

Suddenly Alan wanted to hit her, but Alice put her hand on his shoulder. He knew she knew he was thinking about his mother, and he almost hated her for it. He was pissed off at himself, too, for getting like this—it wasn't like he'd seen her after the accident or anything—it was just his stupid imagination. Instinctively, he shrugged Alice off. "Forget it," he said. "Let's just go get lunch."

He was in a foul mood all the way to the Center to get pizza, and in a worse one when they came back and discovered that he'd forgotten his keys. They tried the front door and the side door and the French doors that led into the living room and the back door of the greenhouse, but all was locked fast. It was too cold to sit on the patio furniture making small talk until Trish came back at three, and Alan declared himself too tired to walk anywhere else.

"I'll just break a window," he announced.

"You can't just break a *window*," Alice told him. "Your father will have a total cow."

This was an advantage that had not yet occurred to Alan; he paused.

"You think so?"

"What do you mean, do I think so? What do *you* think he's going to say when he comes back and finds that you've broken a window?"

"I don't know—he didn't say anything, last time."

"That was totally different! Come on, Keith, tell him. He can't break a window! It's crazy!"

"Come on, Alan—don't be an idiot," Keith obliged. "We can kill time in the Center. Oh, stop looking so nervous, Agnes! He's not going to break the window."

That sealed it. Before Alan really knew what he was doing, he was taking a running leap at the window. He kicked his Doc Martens right at the crystal pane and shattered it.

"Cool," he said in the silence that followed the tinkling rain of glass shards.

They all stood staring at the broken pane and the litter of glass on the shiny floor of the living room, listening to the increasingly frantic whine of the burglar alarm. Agnes had gone very white, but Alice was looking angry. Keith and Jethro looked at each other, as if trying to decide which expressions to plaster on their faces, but Alan didn't care. An incredible rush of adrenaline was surging through his veins. His fevered brain saw the moment over and over: the pane shattering into pieces, the sighing crash. "We should have filmed that!" he mourned. "Why didn't we film it?"

"Because the camera was inside," answered Alice drily. "That was why you had to break the window, remember?"

"Let's do it again! We should *totally* film that! Did you see it? It was *awesome!*"

Alice put her hand firmly on Alan's shoulder and maneuvered him toward the window. "All right, wild guy," she said, "go turn off the alarm before the police come and cart you away, okay?"

They sat in the kitchen drinking hot chocolate while Agnes swept up the glass and found a piece of cardboard to put over the hole. Alan was still tingling with the excitement of the crash, but the others were looking very nervous as they tried to figure out how to leave before Alan's father came home. Agnes was looking positively green.

"I guess we have to go," said Alice eventually. "Are you sure you'll be okay?"

"Okay?" Alan nearly shouted. "Okay? I feel *great!*" It had been an incredible moment, watching that glass break. More than anything he wished he could remember that crash forever.

He was still thinking about it when Trish came heavily up the stairs.

"Alan," she said, leaning against his door frame. He didn't turn; he was watching what they had filmed that day. "Alan, do you want to tell me something?"

"I broke a window."

"Yes, I observe that you broke a window. Would you like to tell me *why?*"

"Got locked out. That's all it was, *this* time." He didn't take his eyes from the TV: there was Jethro, rolling stiffly down the stairs. It actually looked pretty stupid, not at all like he'd imagined when he'd planned the scene. Maybe he didn't really have a calling to be the next Hitchcock or whoever. He yawned.

"Alan Green, that is a ridiculous reason to break a window. Are you telling me that you . . ." Two minutes later he couldn't remember what she had said to him; her voice was like the calling of crows in the morning when you're trying to sleep. "I thought after the shotgun incident you and Keith were done with this sort of stunt, *caw caw caw* . . ." Alan yawned, but Trish went on and on. ". . . when your father gets home . . ." A little thrill ran through Alan then, the way a bullfighter must feel at the mention of a bull. He *wanted* his father to come home and see the broken window and hear his son say "I got locked out" with an artful shrug of indifference. But when his father finally came back at nine the next night, he listened to Alan's explanation with a shrug of his own, and went upstairs to his study with a cocktail. The ice cubes clinked in the heavy glass as he walked by Alan, and that was all that was said on the subject.

In English the next day, they were reading the Harlem Renaissance poet Countee Cullen. They were supposed to break up into groups and discuss the poems, and Alan could tell from the swiveling heads and nervous looks that no one wanted to be partnered with Juliet.

He considered this. Why should it be embarrassing to discuss a black poet's work with a person who happened to be black? It was just like when they read about Mormonism in fifth-grade history and everyone was embarrassed to talk about it in front of Elsie Martin—or the way people got all weird about mothers in front of him, like he was going to burst into tears or something. He didn't really know why this should be true, but it was. Juliet's blackness was always there, standing between her and the others because they wanted it not to be there. He noticed how often they mentioned black things around her, name-dropping black musicians or black movies or black celebrities as if to signal to her that they didn't mind her blackness. Jethro was especially stupid about it. "You know who I really like," he'd said to her out of the blue one day, "*James Brown.* He's so effin' *cool*"—and for a moment, Alan had felt as sick as if he'd said such an idiotic thing himself. Now he moved his chair backwards a little and tried to catch Mrs. Perry's eye. *Put me with Juliet,* he signaled to her. *I won't be stupid.*

And Mrs. Perry, who was sometimes *perceptive, astute,* and *discerning,* seemed to get the message. Five minutes later Alan and Juliet were in the back of the room, huddled over their handouts.

"You should have come to make the movie," he said to her, by way of hello.

"Sorry. I had class, like I told you, and on Sunday my parents took me to the ballet downtown."

"Did it have any breaking windows in it?"

"No," said Juliet, smiling. "Just dancing." He noticed she was rolling the handout up and smoothing it out again with sweaty palms; she looked totally nervous.

"What's wrong?" he asked her.

"It's just that I hate this sort of assignment. I'm *useless* with poetry."

"Don't worry about it," Alan said gallantly. "This is my secret superpower."

She raised an eyebrow. "You're a poet?"

"No," he scoffed. "Just a critic." He spread out the poems on the desk and began.

He hadn't lied: reading poetry really was his secret power—a power because he could always find something to say about a poem, and secret because he wasn't an idiot. There was nothing *unobtrusive* about understanding poetry, but, hey, you were stuck with the talents you were given. Aquaman probably wished he could do something better than just talk to jellyfish, too—but there you had it. He bent over the poems.

"This is going to be easy," he announced after a

moment. "*Man*, is this dude angry." And he showed her the places where Cullen described the despair of waiting for racism to end: "'Dead men are wisest, for they know / How far the roots of flowers go, / How long a seed must rot to grow.' Cool. I like that."

"I don't get it."

"Sure you do. Look—he's saying something's going to happen *someday*—the roots are going down and down, and *someday* those rotting seeds are going to grow—but look how cool and cynical he is about it. It's like all going to happen after we're dead and rotted. I like this dude. He's totally cool."

"I still don't get what he's waiting for."

"I don't know—justice maybe . . . or the time when a black man could be a famous poet."

"I guess it happened—all these rich white kids reading his poems now."

"And just liked he guessed, he's dead. But look, look—Perry will love this—look how he uses the language of waiting like the language of death. This whole poem is so cold, so detached. Look here at the end, where he says the dead are 'Wrapped in their cool immunity.' It's like he wants to be dead so he doesn't have to feel. *Cool immunity*. I like that."

"A phrase *you* should understand," she said archly.

If Alice had said it, he would have been flattered. Coming from Juliet, it stung. It was like she was telling him that cool immunity was one thing when it was trying to lay to rest dangerous passions, and quite another when it covered no passions at all. He shook his head and turned to the last poem, "From the Dark Tower." He read it to himself, twice, to make sure he understood where the words went, and then he read it out loud to Ballerina Juliet:

We shall not always plant while others reap
The golden increment of bursting fruit,
Not always countenance, abject and mute,
That lesser men should hold their brothers cheap;
Not everlastingly while others sleep
Shall we beguile their limbs with mellow flute,
Not always bend to some more subtle brute;
We were not made eternally to weep.

The night whose sable breast relieves the stark
White stars is no less lovely being dark,
And there are buds that cannot bloom at all
In light, but crumple, piteous, and fall;
So in the dark we hide the heart that bleeds,
And wait, and tend our agonizing seeds.

Even Juliet could understand the thrust of the poem, how it, like the others, spoke of the day black people would no longer be oppressed, but Alan showed her the painful parts of the poem, how the line *We were not made eternally to weep* suggested they *were* made to weep, at least for a while; how the word *eternally* made that day of release a long way off.

Then he turned his attention to the second stanza, the sextet, and showed her the implicit criticism of the idea that white was good and black bad: how the *white stars* (usually accounted lovely by poets) were here diminished by being *stark*, and how the night was described in warm, maternal tones both in the word *breast* and the word *sable* (which, having been looked up in the dictionary, turned out to be a kind of warm, dark fur). And this, taken with Cullen's description of prejudiced whites as *lesser men*, showed a quiet rejection of the world imposed upon him. But he wasn't really sure if the *agonizing seeds* in the last line should refer to the painful sort of art Cullen was creating himself, or the agony that would come when (in the words of poet Langston Hughes) "the dream deferred" exploded instead of drying up like a raisin in the sun.

"I could never do that," Juliet said when he was done.

"What, explode?"

"No—read the poem like that. You paid attention to every word. I *never* would have thought to think about *stark* and *sable* like that. Or tried to figure out the metaphors. It's like it was a code, and you were decoding it or something."

"I told you, this is my secret talent."

"Well, Alan Green, I misjudged you. You're not as shallow as I thought."

She was wrong about that, but he sure as hell wasn't going to point it out. He let her do the talking in their presentation, and was ridiculously pleased when Perry gave the A to both of them.

Juliet ran out of class as soon as the bell rang, but Alan hung back, just in case Mrs. Perry wanted to drop any more compliments his way. She was stuffing her papers into her ugly tapestry bag and looked up to see him there.

"You did a good job today," she said.

Alan shrugged.

"I thought Countee Cullen might speak to you."

Alan shrugged again.

Mrs. Perry rolled her eyes at him. "Mr. Green," she said, shaking her head. "You are a cipher to me. It is a mystery how you can see so much in poetry, and yet try so hard to feel so little in life. I do always hold the secret hope that you yourself will be a great poet someday. . . ."

"Me?" he hooted. "*I'm* not going to be a poet!"

"Not if you poison your life with cynicism," Mrs. Perry answered. "And that wasn't a compliment, Alan."

But he knew it really was a compliment. He made as if he were going to give her an aw-shucks punch on the arm, then sauntered, satisfied, out of her classroom, wrapped in his cool immunity, with his cold *sang-froid* that never boiled with any emotions at all flowing through his veins like rivers of ice. He strode through the halls, his Doc Martens clunking on the vomit-colored carpet, and felt how very cool he was. Nothing bothered him, not even when he came around the corner and saw Kaufman getting slammed up against the wall of lockers. Rory Frankel stopped for a moment to see who it was and, seeing Alan (who after all had done his time in the ring circling Richard Paas), nodded curtly and slammed Kaufman's head back against the locker. Kaufman flinched, and Alan hurried on. His cold blood was pounding in his ears.

USUALLY ALAN'S FATHER spent the whole weekend with his girlfriend, but that following Sunday he was home for dinner. For the first time in a long time, they had the usual Sunday dinner of steak, rice pilaf, and salad, just like his mother used to make. To Alan, the taste of the meal had always been the desperate taste of free time slipping away towards the interminable week. Back when he had just started at Josiah Quincy, before he'd bolstered his cloak of invisibility by adding Jethro and Keith to his posse, even the thought of rice pilaf and steak would make him want to puke.

He was over that now; the smell of the grilled steaks lured him downstairs without Trish having to call him twice. His father was still on the patio, standing in front of the gas grill that was his pride and joy, and the delicious aroma of seared meat came through the French doors. Alan stood in the foyer for a moment before going to the table. He felt very comfortable in his big, clean house, and his nice, clean clothing, with the smell of high-quality beef dancing delightfully on the air. He was glad they were rich.

Trish had set three places on the long table in the dining room, as she always did when Alan's father was home for supper—he didn't like the informality of the kitchen where she and Alan ate. In the beginning, soon after the funeral, Trish would try to get Alan to eat with her in the dining room and have improving conversation. One good thing about her, though, was that she learned fast—now they ate in the kitchen, and when Alan didn't want to talk, he didn't. But all bets were off when his father was home.

Now Alan's father opened a beer and drank half of it before tearing into his steak, cutting a piece and eating it with quick, jerky movements. He was the fastest eater Alan had ever seen, cutting a piece of meat and shoveling it into his mouth without even transferring his fork from the left hand to the right. He had an enormous mouth, too—he could fit a whole red potato into it at once and eat a Big Mac in two bites.

"So what's happening at school?" he asked, jabbing at his meat.

"Usual crap."

"And who's this Juliet who called you?"

Alan put down his fork. "*Juliet* called me?" he asked.

"Didn't you see the message? It was right next to the phone. She wanted the assignment for English, but said she'd get it somewhere else."

Alan sawed at his steak, his face bent over his plate. It was ridiculous; he was blushing like an idiot.

"So," Trish said, passing around the salad. "Who is she, Alan? I don't think I've heard you mention a Juliet before . . ."

"She's just a girl in my class."

"*Just* a girl, huh," his father commented, looking at Alan's red face. "Did you ask her out yet?"

Desperately, Alan turned to Trish.

"Don't tease him, Mitch," she said. "Come on, Alan, help me clear the table." She gave him a sympathetic, *understanding* smile. Alan scowled back. She was pissing him off more than usual. His father was just trying to needle him on principle, but Trish thought that she had him all figured out, and that was infinitely more annoying.

All through English the next day Alan sat looking at Juliet's neck and screwing up his courage. He had finished his reading response ages ago, and now he sat trying out phrases of a note to her. *I heard you called*—scratch it out. *What are you doing this*—scratch scratch scratch scratch scratch. It was hopeless, ridiculous. He could write a billion quick sentences on Robert Frost, but he could not produce a single sentence he could show to Juliet Jones. It was as if his courage and resolve were made up of a platoon of poorly disciplined soldiers; they all deserted when they saw her, taking Alan's ability to speak coherently with them.

At last he just grabbed her, hoping some of what he said would come out in English.

"Hey—what are you doing this afternoon? It's not Tuesday or Thursday, so you can't have dance class."

Juliet raised an eyebrow. "You pay attention to my schedule?"

"I pay attention. Can you come over? I'm ready to be your tutor."

"My *tutor*?"

"On being a usual, idle, time-wasting American youth."

Juliet paused, hesitated. He had noticed that when she thought, she flexed and unflexed her right foot. She flexed it now.

"I have to be home by five," she said. "I have to practice before dinner."

"No problem," said Alan joyously. "I'll get you home before you turn into a pumpkin." And then, to compound the mortification of the old-lady cutesiness of the phrase *before you turn into a pumpkin*, he flushed bright red.

"What do you mean, you're busy?" Alice demanded, when Alan caught up with her in the hall.

"I have something to do."

"I knew what you *meant*," said Alice, more snottily than he'd ever heard her. "English is my first language, in case you don't remember. I meant, *why* are you busy?"

"I just have plans."

She sniffed. "You have *plans*."

"I invited someone over."

Alice said nothing, like she was waiting for him to tell her more. But Alan had had years of practice at the waiting game—she wasn't going to get him that way.

"So I'll see you tomorrow," he said at last.

"Yeah, unless *I* have plans," she retorted.

Alan stopped and stared at her. "What are you, like, jealous? It's not like we have to see each other every afternoon."

"We *don't* see each other every afternoon," she said, the flush rising on her cheeks. "I'm just saying—"

"Oh, come on, Al, don't be like that. You look like your mother when she's having a conniption fit."

"Forget it. I'm just saying, it's funny how this is the first time you've ever . . ."

"If it's the first time, why are you so upset? It's not like I do it all the time."

"Aw, forget it, you putz." She stalked off. He could see by the way she was gesticulating to Agnes that she was really offended. Well, it wasn't like he needed to explain himself to her. It wasn't like they were goddamn *married*.

He found Juliet waiting for him by the lockers.

"Where's everyone else?"

"What do you mean, everyone else?"

"Your little gang. Keith. Jethro. The twins."

He shrugged. "They're busy. And you shouldn't call them 'the twins.' They hate that."

"Okay," Juliet said. She seemed a little less confident

now that she knew that she was going to Alan's alone. She flexed her foot and waited for him to talk.

"Well, let's go, then," he said. He directed her to the back door so they wouldn't have to pass the others, leading her chivalrously across the field behind the school. On the way, he entertained ridiculous fantasies of laying down his coat over puddles so she could walk across dry-shod. But the dry October weather thwarted romance, and in the end all he could do was to open the door gallantly as he welcomed her into the entryway.

Juliet turned around in a slow semicircle, taking in the painting of sepia-colored trees and buildings.

"What's *this*?" she asked, eyebrow arched, pointing to the collegiate scene.

"Harvard Yard. You know, at Harvard."

"I've heard of it."

"My father," he said by way of explanation, and led her into the foyer.

She walked past him, tall and graceful. She looked so good there in that formal space that he watched her with pride as she took a quick step up and down on the wide, red-carpeted, *Gone with the Wind* staircase that led to the second floor. She looked down at the black-and-white-checkered marble floor, and then through the French doors to the dining room and the greenhouse beyond.

"Oh," she said, "I get it now. You're *rich*."

This was a slap in the face.

"*I'm* not rich," Alan protested. "It's my *father* who's rich."

"Same difference." She walked so softly her feet hardly made a sound on the floor. Walking behind her, Alan heard his own lonely footsteps echoing as if he were alone.

"He doesn't give me whatever I want, if that's what you mean," Alan said. "I mean, Alice and Agnes get more allowance than I do."

Juliet still said nothing. She walked around the empty, echoing foyer and peered curiously up the stairs.

"Are your parents home?" she asked.

"My parents are never home. My aunt's probably out grocery shopping—she usually does that Mondays. Come on—let's get a drink. We have usually have Cokes and stuff."

"I don't drink it."

She followed him to the kitchen, looking around the expensive stainless-steel appliances and the fancy Spanish tiles, and sat down at the table. She accepted a glass of water from Alan and looked at him expectantly. "So your aunt lives here?"

Alan shrugged. "My father spends a lot of time at his girlfriend's, so he wants someone to stay with me and make sure I don't burn the house down or shoot anyone or anything. My mother's dead."

"I didn't know," she said. "About your mother, I mean. I'm sorry."

This was surprising. Usually, when people found out about his mother, they changed the subject so fast it was like they'd opened a bathroom door to find the stall was occupied. It was pretty comical, actually, to see how quickly they tried to get out of it—as if a packed suitcase suddenly appeared next to them, and they were standing there, ticket in hand, *see-you-later, don't-forget-to-write*. But here was Juliet, not looking away, not changing the topic, her sorrowful eyes inviting him to talk.

"It's okay," he said gruffly. "It was a while ago. I'm fine now." Involuntarily, he looked down at the tiny scars that crisscrossed the fingers of his left hand.

"How did she die?"

"What?"

"I said, how did she die?"

Alan shook his head as if to clear it and said, "Uh, God took out a hit on her."

"What?"

"Drunk driver. She was killed by a drunk driver."

Now *he* wanted her to change the subject; he really didn't want to talk about it. Mercifully, she understood. But still, she pressed him.

"So, do you mind your father not being here?"

This one was easy to field.

"Why should I mind? It's not like I miss him." But suddenly he didn't really want to talk about that, either. "So, do you want to come see my room?"

"I guess," she said.

He didn't know why he led her up the back stairs, unless it was because he didn't want her to comment on the plantation-style staircase in the foyer. He had never been embarrassed by his house before. It was just his house, strange and empty but comfortable and clean smelling.

People had laughed at it before, of course—laughed at the empty rooms and the pretentious greenhouse, but he had never felt such disapproval as came shimmering off Juliet Jones. The back stairs, at least, were plain and unpretentious. The walls were painted beige, and they were carpeted with gray industrial carpet like the stairs in any apartment building. But Juliet sniffed.

"*Servants'* stairs, huh?" she asked.

This was not how he wanted her to react. He began to dread the moment he showed her his room. He had always been proud of it—he liked the posters and the way his stereo and CD collection totally filled the nook in the corner, but now the whole afternoon seemed ill-advised.

"So what do you like to do?" she asked. "Besides *hang out*, I mean."

"I've been making movies."

"Really? Are they any good?"

Alan considered.

"Naw, not really. They're pretty much a waste of tape."

She smiled then. Emboldened, Alan went on.

"And I have this spy group. I mean, it sounds dorky, but it was a lot of fun . . . we even predicted the governor's assassination."

"Really?"

"Sure. Well, not exactly. But we did predict something was going to happen. Ask Keith and Alice—they were there."

For a moment, he thought she wasn't as disgusted as usual with him. Then she caught a glimpse of the open bathroom door and raised an eyebrow. "You have your own *bathroom?*"

"Uh—it came with the house."

She walked in, appraising the claw-foot tub and the wooden shutters on the window.

"No Jacuzzi?"

"That's in my father's bathroom."

"Right," she said. "Of course. What's that door lead to?"

It had never occurred to him to be embarrassed about the second bedroom. After all, in a house with seventeen rooms and only three people in it, it would have been ridiculous for him not to have at least two rooms to call his own. And with seventeen rooms in the house, it made sense that there should be a den with the enormous TV for Alan's father to watch football on Sundays and also this room where Alan could watch DVDs or play video games with his friends without his father or Trish coming in wanting to watch their own crap.

But now, watching Juliet take in the TV and the pile of DVDs (most of them rented, he wanted to point out) and the two different game systems and the scattered cartridges on the floor, he felt himself blushing. If anyone else had made him feel this way, he would have blasted them with his sarcastic indifference. But somehow, watching Juliet's cool appraisal of his life, Alan felt her disapproval burn like napalm on his skin. He found he had nothing to say at all.

"Another TV," she observed.

"My father likes to be able to watch TV whenever he wants to," Alan explained.

"Of course," she said pointedly. "My father does, too."

This was too much. "Look," Alan spluttered. "I'm sorry if I disgust you, but it's not my—"

"No," Juliet interrupted. "You don't *disgust* me. This just explains a lot."

"Explains what?"

"It explains why you don't have any direction. You're like . . . you're like a veal calf—or a stuffed goose. You've been given everything you could possibly want even before you want it, and it makes you soft."

Alan snorted at this. He imagined the list of adjectives Mrs. Perry used to describe him, and *soft* was nowhere on it. *Cynical, misanthropic, disaffected,* wrapped in cool immunity—that's what he was. Even his enemies at school knew it. Why didn't she?

"I'm not soft," he informed her.

"Your *desire* is soft," she answered. "You have no passion. There's nothing you'd fight for—nothing you'd *die* for. You don't have great loves. I can't imagine anything that would set your heart on fire." Her brown eyes flashed with her inner flame, and it seared him. She didn't hate him, after all. She just felt sorry for him, and that was a thousand times worse.

"I just haven't found it yet," he said inadequately.

"You aren't looking, either," she said. "And why should you? Your life is defined by comfort. You're—what's that word? You know, a person who lives for pleasure?"

"Okay," he said hotly, "so I'm a hedonist. What's so damn wrong with that?"

"Because real pleasure comes from caring about something so much it's the only thing worth living for—worth fighting for, worth suffering for."

He had no idea what she was saying, beyond that he was being insulted, and he cast about for some way to prove her wrong. Something to fight for—well, he had fought Richard Paas. But that had been over nothing, not even honor. He had fought only so he would not need to fight later; he had fought to avoid pain and humiliation. He tried to imagine what he *would* fight for. What about Alice? She was certainly important; she had been his best friend for years. He would certainly go find Kellerman to break up any fight that threatened her. He might even jump in and break up the fight himself so long as it was only a fistfight and he had some chance of getting out of there without getting clocked on the head. But Juliet was right. Alice was as close to a passion as he had, aside from the strange feelings he had for Juliet, and he could not say he would die for *her*. But then again, maybe that was asking too much of a person. Take his father, for example. Alan couldn't imagine anything *he* would die for, but no one could ever accuse *him* of being soft.

Since there was no way to answer her, he got angry. "Fine," he said. "When you're done insulting me, what should we do? Do you just want to go home?"

"Do *you* want me to go home?"

"No, I want you to *want* to be here."

Juliet looked at him, and improbably, she smiled. Her smile was so beautiful it hurt Alan's heart. The lips broke open, showing a flash of her crooked teeth on her lovely dark face, and her eyes crinkled gently in the corners.

"I want you to want me to want to be here," she said. "I'm staying."

They watched cartoons together, on the couch. Alan felt he had never been so aware of another person beside him. She was very tall. She had three or four inches on him standing up, but sitting down she towered over him. Alan kept the pillow over his lap and wrapped his arms around his knees, trying not to touch her. He was suddenly very aware of her smell, a smell of Wisk detergent and maybe talcum, and her own smell under it that reminded him irrelevantly of grapes. She was very still, with her ramrod posture, but after a while she stretched out one leg and then the other and began pointing her toes and flexing her muscles as if working out some sort of routine. But she liked the tape he showed her, and the next one, and then, with much portentous introduction, he popped in the movie he'd made, giving her the detailed director's commentary. She laughed a lot, heartily and happily, and suddenly she fell against him and put her head on his shoulder. At that moment, Alan knew that if she hadn't been wrong before when she'd said he didn't care about anything, she was certainly dead wrong now.

ZXY CHAPTER NQR

1 2 4 5 7 5 0 4 5 2 7 6 5

MONDAY WAS THE SECOND NIGHT in a row his father was home for dinner, and Alan suddenly felt a surge of impossible hope that he was breaking up with his girlfriend. But no hidden tear shone in his father's eye, no lump appeared in his throat, and he appeared every inch as self-satisfied as usual. But it didn't matter. Alan was in a fine mood.

"Good day today, Alan?"

"Great day."

"Good," his father said. "Listen, I want to talk seriously about something." As if on cue, Trish stood up and began clearing the plates; she shut the pocket doors behind her as she disappeared into the kitchen.

"Let's go for a walk," his father said, standing up and stretching. "Go get your coat."

"Why walk?" asked Alan, trying to squelch his creeping sense of dread. "Why not sit here?"

"We're walking," his father repeated.

Slowly, Alan shrugged on his leather jacket and waited for his father to zip up his own. The creeping dread was up to his stomach now, a leaden weight.

"Your jacket's getting a little tight around the shoulders," his father observed, reaching over and touching Alan's arm. "Growing, aren't you?"

"Despite the best intentions of the universe."

"Think about trying out for football? You're getting the build for it."

"Not unless I can play under general anesthesia."

"Well, anyway, the jacket's getting too small. We should get you a new one. Maybe next weekend."

Alan rolled his eyes.

"Just out with it, will you, Mitch? Let's cut the crap. What's going on?"

This was a little ruder than he usually got away with. The angry white dents Alan used to fear more than anything appeared on either side of his father's nose.

"Cut the crap?" his father repeated dangerously. "You want me to *cut the crap?* All right, then, Alan, I will. I talk straight in business and I'll talk straight with you. Cheryl and I want to get married."

This was so unexpected and so very dreadful that Alan almost staggered.

"So?" he choked, when he could manage it.

"We're getting married," his father repeated. "And I want to make myself clear. Cheryl is coming to live in the house. *My* house. With me. I have been sensitive to your feelings for a long time—"

"Oh, have you?" Alan exploded. "I guess you're right—Mom's already been dead two whole years. *Two years.* So what do you want from me, the goddamn Nobel Sensitivity Prize?"

"Two years," his father repeated. "And in those two years you have not shown one instant of respect, much less acceptance, of my relationship with Cheryl. I have tried to give you space. I have not forced Cheryl on you. How many times have the two of you been in the same room? Three? Five?"

"Eight," corrected Alan.

"Eight," his father repeated. "Hardly onerous. Eight times in two years. I have not brought her over for Thanksgiving dinner, not for your birthday, not for the Fourth of July or the anniversary of your mother's death or any other time I thought would be painful to you. I have tried to respect your feelings, warped and sophomoric as they may be, but now I have to be straight with you. Despite your myopic beliefs to the contrary, I am not yet a doddering, drooling old man in diapers. To put it bluntly, your mother is dead and I am not."

Alan was still reeling. He had lost his composure and with it his advantage. "Look," he said, raising his voice to keep out the tremor, "I'm sorry I get in your way, but I will remind you that it wasn't *me* who decided you should have a kid. That one is not my fault."

"I didn't give up my inalienable rights just because I became a parent," his father said. "I didn't give up the right to have a life. I am not abrogating my responsibilities, Alan. I have carefully weighed my desires and your needs. When you made it clear you didn't want to spend time with Cheryl, I brought Trish to stay with you so I could go to Cheryl's instead of bringing her home. I have not ignored my responsibilities as a father. I—"

"You're always telling me how smart you are," Alan broke in. Fury made him cold to the core, and he didn't care what he said. "You're always telling me how you went to *Harvard* and how you destroy other CEOs and clean up at the poker table and all that, but you totally don't get it. It's not that I didn't want Cheryl in the *house*. I didn't want Cheryl around, *period*. You forgot about Mom not two minutes after she was dead!" He paused, breathing hard, and then he burst out, "God! I wish *you'd* been in that car instead of her!"

He had gone too far.

"How dare you speak to me like that!" his father threatened. "You spoiled son of a bitch, if I were my father, I would belt you one right now."

"Yeah, *that* would prove what a great father you are."

"That's it," his father announced. "I'm goddamn fed up with this. It ends right here. You are grounded for two weeks. Trish will pick you up after school and you will come straight home. No friends, no TV, no e-mail. I will take away your cell phone and games and your DVD player until the two weeks are up. Trish will make sure you use your computer only for schoolwork. Don't look at me like that—I don't care if you hate me right now. You've been spoiled long enough—it's time you learn childhood is not free from responsibilities. In these self-righteous, entitled times I may seem like a crappy father to you, but *you* are certainly a poor excuse for a son in any generation."

They stood there for a moment, steely gray eyes staring into steely gray eyes, and then Alan's father stalked off through the dead and swirling leaves. Alan watched him go. He did not start to cry until his father had entirely disappeared around the corner.

"What happened to you? I called you twice last night and your aunt wouldn't put me through."

Alan looked up from his congealing lunch. There was Juliet, standing next to him, her own lunch tray balanced on her hip. The miserableness of the night before had blocked her from his mind, but now the light pressure of her hand on his shoulder had the opposite effect. She took up so much of his attention he almost forgot the others at the table.

"I got grounded," he told her.

"Well, that much is obvious. The question is, what did you go and get grounded for?"

"I'm a bonehead, I guess," said Alan dejectedly.

"Can you e-mail?"

"No."

"Then I'll just have to figure out how to get messages to you in your imprisonment."

Alice gave a snort then. "For chrissakes, Alan," she interrupted. "Would you invite her to sit down, already? Hey, sit down, will you? I'm guessing you're Juliet. I'm Alice Parker and this is Agnes, my sister, and these are Keith and Jethro and I'm getting a crick in my neck just looking up at you."

Alan flushed, but Juliet sat down. Alice went on obnoxiously, as if the conversation were all about her: "What I don't understand, Alan, is why you *try* to piss him off. You know he's going to ground you. . . ." This was the sort of reasonableness that made her entirely annoying. Didn't she see Juliet wanted to talk to him?

"What was I supposed to do?" he defended himself. "He wants to get married again."

"I'm sorry," Juliet broke in, "but I don't get it. What's wrong with him getting married?"

This was just what Alice had been saying all along, but it was somehow less annoying in Juliet's mouth.

"Well, it's a slap in the face to Alan's mother . . ." Keith tried to explain.

"And it's like a friggin' slap in the face to Alan. Like what if they have like another effin' kid?"

"So what if they have another kid?" Alice asked, looking over to Agnes. "It's nice to have a sibling."

"It's not a *sibling*," Jethro corrected her. "It's like a new baby that your father like cares about more than you because his wife cares about it more than you, and suddenly you're like the full-time babysitter. I only see my father like on Thursdays and every other weekend, and I like babysat five times last month."

"At least he *pays* you," Keith put in. "My stepsister, Katie, she has to take care of her half brother *every afternoon*, for free."

"Well, at least you won't have to worry about that, Al," snorted Alice. "Who's going to trust *you* with a baby?"

They all laughed, even Juliet. Alan's cool immunity went up in flames as he glared at Alice. Who was she, to laugh at him in front of Juliet like that?

"Look, Alan," she went on, in her annoying, grating way, "we all know your dad's a prick—we've said it a hundred times. But the point is since you *know* he's a prick, why do you do things that will set him off?"

It was easy for her to say, with her perfect parents and her easy life. She didn't understand what it was like to be him.

"Come on, Juliet," he said. "Let's go."

"Uh, bye," said Juliet to the others. Alan said nothing as he dumped his tray into the garbage. He did not turn around to see Alice staring after him. *Who's going to trust you with a baby?* indeed. Sometimes he couldn't even stand her.

He found the note from Juliet in his poetry book; she must have sneaked it in during English. It was funny that she was so graceful but her handwriting was so dumb and girlie. But the words of comfort in his captivity were like a saw baked into a prisoner's loaf of bread.

Call the time (617-637-JAIL) at 1:00 a.m., she wrote, *and I'll call your call waiting and the phone won't ring.* SYNCHRONIZE YOUR WATCHES **NOW**. *Until then, Prisoner 666—Agent 4X35.*

All that evening, when he was doing his homework under Trish's watchful eye, he felt the note in his pocket, and smiled. *Alice* had never thought of anything like that. She usually gave him comic books to read during his periods of imprisonment, but she'd never thought of a way to call him before. When Trish went out of the room, Alan took the note out of his pocket and sniffed it; he almost thought he could smell Juliet's talcum and Wisk smell coming off the paper.

It was remarkably hard to stay up until 1:00 without the TV or his DVDs or any of his video games. In the end he had to set his alarm. He had been dreaming when it jangled him awake at 12:45, and bits of the dream flitted before his eyes even as he reached over to turn off the radio. He lay on his back in the dark, trying to recapture the dream images as they dissolved away. Finally, he flipped on the light and went to go find the phone.

"At the tone, the time will be twelve fifty-eight and fifty seconds." *Dong.* "Temperature, thirty-eight Fahrenheit." He took the phone back to his bed and sat down to wait. "At the tone, the time will be twelve fifty-nine, exactly." *Dong.* "Temperature, thirty-eight Fahrenheit." He reached over for the comic book he'd been reading earlier, and his hand fell on the note Juliet had left him. "At the tone, the time will be twelve fifty-nine and ten seconds." *Dong.* Suddenly he reached over and turned off his light. He lay down on the bed, the phone pressing against his ear. "At the tone—" That was it, the beep from call waiting. His heart skipped in his chest.

"You're early," he told her.

"Oh, crud. Did anyone hear?"

"No—I was early, too. We didn't synchronize our watches, I guess."

"*I* synchronized my watch."

"Without doing it together, there's not much *syn*, is there?"

An awkward silence after this.

"How are you doing, in your confinement?"

"Me? I'm fine. Bored out of my skull, but fine."

"I'm sorry about your father. Alice filled me in, a bit, after school. She was the one who figured out the time trick—she's pretty smart, huh?"

"Yeah," said Alan. But he didn't really want to talk about Alice. He was still pissed at her harshness at lunch, her "what sort of an idiot would trust *you* with a baby," and the way she acted like she owned him, lecturing him about how he should act with his father, and he hated the way she kept interrupting his conversations with Juliet.

"Anyway," Juliet went on. "I called for my orders."

"Orders?"

"Yeah—Roberta Bismol asked me to call you."

"*Who?*"

"Roberta Bismol. Isn't that her name? That's what Alice told me her name was. I asked her for something to cheer you up, and she told me about your spy work and Roberta and all." She paused. "They're torturing you in prison, aren't they? That's how you could forget who Roberta is." She was playing all this very awkwardly, like someone who had never played before. He smiled at the sweetness of her trying. After all, it is hard to play when you've had no practice, and Juliet had been doing practice of another kind for a long time now.

"*Bismo*," he corrected huskily. "Her name is Roberta *Bismo*. So you've been briefed on CRAP?"

"A little, Agent 666. Shall I go to the culvert tomorrow, and tell you what I find? You can interpret the data from your prison cell, even if you can't be there to collect it."

He tried to remember the spy name she had given herself in the note.

"Thank you, Agent X543. That will be very kind of you indeed."

"Agent 4X35! Otherwise it doesn't spell anything upside down. It's like Alice's. Get it?"

He hadn't before. "Sexh?" he tried.

"*No*," she said. "Sexy. The four is a *y*."

"Hate to break it to ya, but it's not," said Alan.

"It's not?" she asked sadly. "Oh, it's not. Stupid dyslexia!"

"But do you believe in Dog?"

It took her a minute, but she laughed. She had the most delightful laugh in the world. He pressed the phone closer to his ear, prepared to listen to her forever, when she suddenly told him she had to get off. She hung up, leaving Alan in the dark, holding the phone to his thudding heart with both hands.

A moment later, the phone rang, a jarring, jangling call; he snatched at it just in time to hear his father's receiver clattering off the cradle. It was not Juliet: it was the other line that he had never disconnected.

"At the tone, the time will be one thirty-two, exactly," said the phone, and as his father said, "What the hell . . . ?" Alan hung up the phone very quietly. It was a long time before he fell asleep.

THE WORST PART OF THE RESTRICTION was the mortifying moment when Trish came to escort him home. How humiliating, to have to join in the parade of dorks walking down the hill to the sedans and minivans in the parking lot; to join all the suckers off to lessons or the dentist, or those too lame or too scared to get home by themselves, like Kaufman. *His* mother picked him up every day after school now. She even met him at the door so no one would take a swing at him in the three hundred feet between the school and the car. You could see why. Kaufman had a bit of this cauliflower thing going on with one ear. You'd think he'd be embarrassed to go to school like that, to have to answer all the "What *happened*, dude!"s like Alan had had to do after he put his fist through the window—though that particular incident had only cemented his reputation for cool detachment.

"*What happened to your hand, dude?*"

"*Put it through a window.*"

"Why?"

"*I don't know, man. It was just pissing me off.*"

But what was Kaufman going to say? No one had to ask what had happened because they all knew, and even though they were all secretly scared of Frankel, it didn't exactly make them sympathetic.

And now here was Alan Green, reduced to Kaufman-like status, forced to run the gauntlet of dorks to Trish's car. He didn't speak to her on the way home. Instead he looked out the window, pleasantly reviewing the past six hours. Wednesday was rapidly becoming his favorite day of the week, what with the secret lunch he shared with Juliet. He'd given her the lowdown on the culvert, presenting her with the map he'd drawn in math class, along with a list of what to look for. She went along with it all, offering suggestions and nodding very intelligently, and then, best of all, she'd leaned close as the bell rang and whispered solemnly: "One o'clock?" He'd had to press his hand to his thudding heart to be able to manage a nod back.

That afternoon the phone rang at four-thirty. Alan could hear Trish get up heavily from the chair where she had been reading and pad down the hall. A few minutes later he heard her coming towards his room.

"That was your friend Juliet," she said. "I wish you'd tell your friends you're on restriction. It's the second time she's called, and I don't think it should be my job to have to explain why you can't come to the phone. . . ."

"Isn't that the job of the jailer?"

"I'm not your *jailer*, Alan," Trish explained patiently. "I'm your aunt, and I'm here for *you*, even if you mulishly refuse to see it."

"Then give me the phone."

Trish sighed. "Oh, forget it, Alan. You can be really thickheaded, can't you? I'm asking you if you want to talk about your father."

"*No*, I don't want to talk about my father."

"About Cheryl, then."

"*No*, I don't want to talk about Cheryl."

"I don't know how I feel about them getting married, either, you know," Trish said, sitting down next to Alan on the bed. "I'm not even sure what I'm going to do."

Alan looked up.

"What are you talking about?" he asked. Immediately he realized his tactical error. *Retreat, retreat, abort, abort!* He had given her an opening.

"I'm not going to stay here when I'm not needed, you know. I was just here for this . . . period of adjustment. When you and your father and Cheryl are . . . *adjusted*, I can finally go home."

Come again? He had not anticipated this.

"What do you mean?" he burst out. "This *is* your home!"

"This is where I *live*, Alan, but it's not my *home*. And Cheryl's going to live here soon. She'll want to make it into *her* home, the home she wants, and she's not going to want another woman rattling around in it. She's going to want to decorate it and fill it up with *her* things and make it a home for the three of you as a family. That's why

I haven't decorated it, like your father's asked me to. That's not a job for a sister. It's a job for a wife."

"Are you trying to get me mad?" Alan demanded. "You know I don't want to talk about her being here!"

"I'm not trying to get you mad," said Trish evenly. "I'm trying to get you to realize that Cheryl's going to live here, whether you like it or not, and that the next few years are going to be a lot easier for you if you make the best of it. Cheryl's a very nice person, Alan. She is not your mother and she's not going to try to be your mother, but she is not a monster just because she fell in love with your father."

"Why not?" Alan growled. "My father's a monster."

Trish stood up. "I would tell you not to make this harder than it already is," she sighed, "except that I suspect you can't help it."

At five to one that night, he called the time again, waiting through the infinite repetition of the time and temperature until Juliet's call clicked in. She was whispering so quickly and excitedly he could barely understand what she was saying.

"Slow down, slow down," he said. "What, are you speaking Serbo-Croatian? I can't understand a word of what you're saying."

She stopped whispering, which helped. *"They were there, Alan!"* she said urgently. "The *Boss* was there, and the *Henchman* was there, and the white Ford Probe with the CPR 1 *plate* was there and they hit me on the *head* with a package of cigarettes."

"What do you mean, they hit you on the head?"

"I mean, the Boss threw them over the edge. He *would* have hit me if I'd been sitting three feet over, but then again, if I'd been sitting three feet over, he would have seen me, and oh, Alan! I'm *glad* he didn't see me."

"Did you hear what they were saying?"

"That's what I wanted to tell you! They were talking about a *license* and a *fee!* They were talking about *money,* Alan! They were talking about a payoff!"

"Juliet," said Alan truthfully, "I could kiss you!"

A pause.

"Why?" she asked.

"Because you're blowing this case wide open. What kind of a fee was it? What kind of license?"

"Well . . . he said it was a dog license. But still!"

"Ah," said Alan wisely. "Clearly, it's all in code. Who meets in the cold to talk about a dog license? What, they don't have phones for that kind of crap?"

"So, what does it mean?"

"Well," mused Alan, warming to his task, "first of all, take the fee—they were probably talking about Fiona Murphy. She was called Fee, you know. Fee-ona."

"She was?"

"That's what my father called her when he talked about her. He was always complaining about her." He paused. "Do you think he's one of the corporate sponsors of CRAP? I wouldn't be surprised."

"But why *dogs*? I don't even know what a dog license is!"

"It's one of those things that hang off the dog collar—a dog tag. But I don't know what it means, not yet—we'll just have to crack that code."

"I'm not very good at those cryptogram puzzles, or anything."

"We'll both work on it."

"Okay, but listen, I have to go to sleep. I have class tomorrow."

"I'll see you in English. Save me a seat."

"Okay, Agent 666. See you in the morning."

"Okay. And Juliet—"

"Yeah?"

"What kind of cigarettes were they?"

"They were American Spirits—you know, the ones with an Indian on them."

"Okay. See you tomorrow."

"Okay."

"Save me a seat—"

"I said I would."

"Okay."

"Okay."

"Hang up, already."

"No, *you* hang up."

"*You* hang up!"

"I don't want to hang up. But I have to. I have to get some sleep."

"We'll hang up at the same time."

"Okay. On three. One, two—"

They hung up together. This time, Alan let the automated voice of Time come on before he severed the connection. When he woke up in the morning, he would have given anything to relive his dreams again.

Juliet had left him an envelope taped to his locker with the empty packet of American Spirit cigarettes in it. This blatant violation of the school's zero-tolerance policy, especially when taken with the note from the exotic Ballerina Juliet, only increased Alan's standing among the nudniks who had their lockers nearby. Alan put the cigarette package in his locker and went off to civics class.

One thing he liked about Mrs. Perry was that she let them choose their own seats. The civics teacher, Dr. Mann, had them in assigned rows, alphabetically—presumably because the vaunted Ph.D. that allowed him to call himself by the pretentious honorific of *Doctor* had not trained him to connect twenty-six faces with twenty-six names. Mrs. Perry knew everyone's name, first and last, and called them by both, depending on her mood. Alan was "Alan" when she was being tender and "Mr. Green" when she was being wry, but most often "Green." She used their last names in a military-like way, which was totally funny, since she was the least military person he could imagine, what with her messy hippy hair and her sentimental tearing up all the time when she read them poetry.

Once Alan had tried a little reciprocity and had called her "Perry" to her face.

"That's *Sergeant* Perry to you, Green, " Mrs. Perry had said, and then she had called him an *enfant terrible*.

Dr. Mann was not like that. He called Alan "Mr. Green" not as a joke but because the only thing more humiliating to him than being a junior high school teacher was being stuck as a junior high school teacher far away from the green cricket fields of Jolly Olde England. Alan couldn't stand him.

The class began, as so many did, with a recap of the textbook reading. Thanks to his enforced solitary confinement, Alan had actually done the assignment, which made Dr. Mann's recitation more tedious than ever. He paid attention just long enough to hear Dr. Mann's usual "And here are some pearls of wisdom to cast before you swine . . ." before sliding his notebook out onto his knees. It wasn't exactly clear to Alan why Dr. Mann thought calling his students pigs would endear him to them, but then again, it wasn't exactly clear to Alan that anything could make Dr. Mann endearing. He tuned out.

He amused himself by writing the words DOG TAG on the outside of his notebook and circling each of the letters with a different-colored pen. He put the letters in alphabetical order: ADGGOT, noticing in passing the fact that ADGT looked like the base pairs in DNA. He wrote down the words GOD TOG DO GAG AGOG TO and TOGA; he thought about the word *tag*; he thought about the word *dog* and its various derogatory connotations with the female sex; he thought about the female sex in general.

Then, apropos of nothing but the brilliance of his own brain, he thought about Fiona Murphy and remembered that the new governor was also female. DOG TAG might just mean that she, too, was tagged for assassination by some female-hating organization like CRAP. And then, thinking about the package of American Freedom cigarettes in his locker, he thought about freedom fighters and right-wing militias and people who might think that ridding the world of liberal female governors might be a good idea. But no, he remembered, American Spirit, not American Freedom. But what was the American Spirit if not Freedom? Clearly, the Boss and his Henchman put their cigarette money where their mouths were. It was clear as the sprouting nose hairs on Dr. Mann's face that their choice of cigarettes declared their allegiance to some radical antigovernment militia. Alan sat up straighter: CRAP was taking new form.

He caught up with Juliet in the hall between classes; in all that sea of short and white, she was easy to pick out. He grabbed her by the arm and let loose with his conclusions.

"So they've tagged Fordham?" she asked in a voice that showed she understood exactly what he meant.

"Who's Fordham?" Alan asked stupidly.

"The acting *gov*ernor, Einstein."

"I didn't know her name. But they tagged her. I'm sure of it."

"Do you think she's in danger?"

"Of *course* I think she's in danger. *You* heard them. The Henchman is getting a fee for tagging her."

The bell was ringing again. They hurried in opposite directions. Alice had saved him a seat in earth science, and he spent most of the class explaining it all to her.

"I'm telling you," he said excitedly. "Juliet and I are totally onto something. DOG TAG. Get it? They're putting the mark on Fordham. She's next."

"Who's Fordham?" asked Keith from the lab table behind them.

"The acting *governor*," Alan said over his shoulder. "And she's been marked for assassination, too. The whole goddamn government's coming down."

"Huh," said Alice. "Maybe you're right, Alan. And if they've tagged her, then they must have some sort of woman-hating agenda. Do you want Agnes and me to go and collect more information? We're not doing anything this afternoon and—"

"Nah," he said, cutting her off. "Juliet and I pretty much have it under control."

Alice was looking stupid; she was opening and closing her mouth like a fish. Then the slow burn of a blush rose up from her chest to her forehead.

"What's with *you*?" Alan asked.

"Forget it. If you don't understand, I'm not going to tell you."

"Okay," said Alan. He turned back to the experiment and looked over their notes. "Hey, check this out—we've discovered a new kind of water that's lighter than ice."

Alice was still blushing. She might even have been about to cry. She turned to Keith and Jethro behind them.

Keith panicked. "Mr. Andrews!" he called out, before Alice could start bawling. "Alice and Alan have discovered that ice is heavier than water!"

Mr. Andrews came over and peered myopically at their apparatus.

"Well, that can't be right," he said.

"That's what I'm saying," said Keith, as if it were his experiment that had gone awry.

"Well, make it work," Andrews said, "or else just use numbers that make ice lighter, or the rest of the experiment will be ruined."

"What, we're supposed to fudge our data?" asked Alice in indignation.

"This isn't exactly rocket science," pointed out Andrews, moving on to the next table.

"I can't believe there ever *is* rocket science, if all the rocket scientists go to schools like this," Alice muttered. Angrily, she began erasing their results. The hard eraser smudged and then tore at the paper, and Alice gave out a little whine of annoyance. Alan wasn't really paying attention. He was retracing the words DOG TAG with his finger, and thinking about the nefarious plotting of the Conspiracy.

■ $\boxed{+}$ ■

That afternoon, against Alan's will, Trish gave Kaufman a ride. Trish was openly disgusted by Alan's consternation. "I'm so sorry, Morris," she said. "Alan isn't usually such a complete boor. He's rarely *free* of boorishness, but . . ."

Kaufman was sitting small and patient in the backseat. "It's all right," he said glumly. "If I could not associate with me, I wouldn't either."

"Oh, don't say that," said Trish quickly. "Don't let Alan make you feel that way. . . ."

"It's not just Alan," Kaufman explained. "It's like the whole universe hates me. That's why I'm taking karate."

"You're taking *karate?*" Alan repeated. There were times Kaufman was such a loser you could hardly blame Rory Frankel for pounding him.

Kaufman pointed up at the sign that towered over the parking lot: VILLAGE KARATE, THE LIBERTY PLAZA DANCE STUDIO, BENSON'S DRUGS, and STORE 24. "Sure, I'm taking karate," he said. "Did you think you were bringing me to dance class?"

It was not for nothing that Secret Agent 666 was the head spy of the SRU—he could put pieces of information together faster than a magnet clings to a refrigerator. Of *course* this was where Juliet danced; she had a Benson's Drugs key chain on her crazy set of keys. A house key, a bike-lock key, and nine key chains, including the one for Benson's Drugs, because it was near where she danced. Alan peered out the window to the bike rack—no, she wouldn't be there yet; the car would make it first. He sent psychic messages to his aunt: *dosomeshoppingdosomeshoppingdosomeshopping.*

The desperation of his desire must have done something to hone his psychic abilities, for after Trish had seen Kaufman safely inside the karate studio, she announced she had to go to the drugstore. Alan trailed behind her, smiling wildly. He liked drugstores, anyway; not as good as stationery stores, but promising for different kinds of pens and notebooks and labels for a spy's filing system. By the time he had convinced Trish to buy him a new mechanical pencil and a tiny notebook, he was sure Juliet was in class.

"Hey," he said with practiced nonchalance, "I know I'm on restriction and all. . . ."

"Yes?" asked Trish suspiciously. She pushed her glasses back up her short nose and stared at him, waiting, her purchases balanced on one hip as she tried to open the sticky passenger-side door.

"Could I look in on the dance studio for a minute?"

"Look in on the *dance studio?*" she repeated blankly. This time he'd done it: she was at a loss for words. *Nonplussed, dumbfounded*; that's what Mrs. Perry would say. "Why—what possible reason could you have for wanting to go into a dance studio?"

What lie could he come up with? He considered, then opted for the truth.

"I have a friend dancing there. I'm not going to try to talk to her," he added hastily. "I've just never seen her dance, that's all."

Trish was still staring at him dubiously.

"I just want to know if she's as good as she says she is," Alan explained.

"All right," Trish agreed reluctantly. "I'll wait here five minutes—no more. Go on in."

The dance studio was aggressively clean, but it could not quite cover the odor of sweat; for all the framed photos of graceful ballerinas in floating tutus, the studio pretty much smelled like his father's gym. Alan peered through the glass windows of the classroom doors. It was easy to see that Juliet was not in the first class, nor in the second. But there she was, in the third, dressed in a black leotard, white tights, and flat pink shoes like the other nine girls in the class, holding on to a barre against the wall with her left hand. Her back was towards him. It was straight and long, and when she raised her right hand over her head in a graceful arch, the back stretched impossibly longer.

Alan stared. The exercises they were doing were dull, tedious—leg out, leg in, arm up, arm down, knees bent, knees straight—but everything Juliet did, she did with indescribable grace and poise. He could tell that her dancing was a cut above everyone else's in the room. While the others poked their legs dutifully to the side, Juliet presented hers, *offered* it; her leg was a little higher, her hips a little more open; it was all done with such ease and beauty that it just barely hid the strength behind it. Pride swelled in Alan's heart—pride in friendship of so spectacular a talent.

He wanted to tell Trish about it in the car, but he couldn't find the words. And besides, he didn't want to get into that whole *girls* and *friends* and *girlfriends* thing that seemed so hard to explain to grown-ups. Instead, they drove on in their usual silence. At last Trish found a bridge to extend towards Alan.

"Did you see your friend?"

"Yeah."

"And was she good?"

"I don't know. I guess so."

"Someone from school?"

"Yeah."

"Alan Green, do you have an inexhaustible supply of uninformative monosyllables? Sometimes it amazes me that you do so well in English."

They drove in silence for a while. Alan liked riding in the car; he liked the way you could talk with someone without trying to figure out what part of their face you were supposed to look at. "Hey—" he said suddenly, before he even knew he was going to ask it. "If my dad—if Cheryl—if they move into the house, will you really leave?"

"Yes, Alan," she said, keeping her eyes fixed on the road. "I'm really going to leave."

"Will you go back to Cincinnati, or will you stay here?"

"I haven't really thought about it. I don't really have anything to do here, you see—I never really settled in, never really found my groove."

This was such a bizarre statement on her part that Alan stared at her, *dumbfounded, nonplussed*. For the first time he had a flash that the indignities of childhood might not disappear miraculously at some magic entry to adulthood. Maybe Trish walked friendless and purposeless in the big corridors of life, a Kaufman in the world of adults. It was an unpleasant thought.

"Aren't you happy here?" he demanded.

"I'm not *un*happy," she answered. "I just liked my life better in Cincinnati. I came out here to help my only nephew adjust after the tragedy that happened to his mother, and help my only brother while he got his life back into order. And now his life's in order, and his son's about as adjusted as he's ever going to be, so my work here is done. It's time for me to ride off into the sunset to the accompaniment of soulful cowboy music."

"Can't you take me with you?"

She laughed then, and rumpled his hair. She drove the rest of the way home with a smile on her face, just as he'd intended; but really, he thought, it wasn't *totally* a joke.

Keith came over later in the afternoon with Alan's math book.

"And what, pray tell, are you doing with Alan's math book?" asked Trish, leaning against the door frame to block Keith's way in.

"Well, ma'am," Keith drawled, "I will confess it was because I took it out of his bag."

"And why, pray tell, did you take Alan's math book out

of Alan's bag?" From the tone of her voice Alan knew that odds were good she would let him in. Improbably, Trish liked Keith; she had once told Alan that of all the bad influences in the world, he was the most amusing. She couldn't bring herself to wish he wasn't friends with Alan.

"I took it to manufacture an excuse," Keith explained.

"You did? And an excuse for what, exactly?" She was laughing now, and had moved out of the door frame so Keith could get a foot into the little hallway: the perimeter was breached.

"An excuse to see you, of course," said Keith gallantly. "Or did you think there's some other reason that we always choose Alan's habitation for our postmaritime rendezvous?"

"Postmaritime?" Trish repeated, laughing. "You don't mean postmeridian, by any chance? Fine! How am I to stand in the way of such intended eloquence? You can have ten minutes with the prisoner, and then it's back to breaking rocks or whatever it is prisoners do these days."

Keith came into the kitchen, holding out the math book and sniffing elaborately. "Got anything to eat?"

"Potato chips."

Keith scraped the chair across the kitchen floor and sat on it backwards. His belly sat on his thighs as he leaned the second of his chins on the back of the chair.

"I saw Juliet dance today," Alan said after a while.

"Ballerina Juliet?"

"Yeah."

"And?"

"She was *unbelievable*."

"You like her, huh?"

Alan shrugged. "She's pretty cool. And she has a good sense of humor."

"Ah," said Keith wisely. "And by that do you mean that you laugh at *her* jokes, or that she laughs at *yours?*"

Alan rolled his eyes. "She laughs at mine, of course," he said.

"Time's up," said Trish, hurrying Keith out the door. He wasn't gone two minutes before he rang the bell.

"I have something else to say to Alan," he announced.

"I can pass on the message."

"Tell him before he proceeds on his adopted route, he might want to speak with Alice."

"Tell him he's wrong," Alan called from the kitchen.

"Wrong about what?" Trish asked when she came back. Alan opened his math book.

"Wrong about Alice. Alice doesn't care what I do."

"I doubt that," said Trish, and she set some onions sizzling in a pan. "I suspect Alice cares quite a bit what you do."

It was strange how suddenly everyone wanted to talk about Alice. That night on the phone she was all Juliet wanted to talk about. Finally she had stopped beating around the bush.

"So," she said. "Tell me about Alice. Is she your girl-friend?"

"*Alice?*" he said. "Are you *kidding?*"

"What about Agnes, then?"

"You'd have to be delusional to think I'd be interested

in *Agnes*. You'd have to be a crack-smoking schizophrenic *psycho* hearing voices in your *head* to think that."

"Okay, then," she giggled. "Is it Jethro? Or that Keith from English?"

"No," Alan laughed. "Not them, either."

"Well, *good*," said Juliet. And then, "But is there some-one?"

"I don't know," said Alan huskily. "Maybe."

"Well," she warned, "tell her not to get her hopes up, because I can be pretty jealous of my friends' time."

And when you thought about it afterwards, as Alan did again and again, there was a lot to be read into that particular conversation.

But maybe, inexplicably, Trish had been right about Alice. All morning Alan had the sense that Alice was waiting to talk to him. She sat beside him quietly and patiently in earth science until Andrews gave the go-ahead to begin the experiment, and then she whispered, "We have to talk."

"What?"

"We have to talk. After school—before Trish picks you up. Meet me by my locker, okay?"

"Why not by my locker?"

"Other people have lockers by your locker."

Alan rolled his eyes, but a dull sense of dread dogged him all day, as if he'd been tapped for another fistfight.

There were too many eighth graders at Josiah Quincy;

some of them had to have lockers in the basement, like the sixth graders. This was the indignity that had befallen Alice. They had teased her about it when she'd gotten her assignment, but it was useful. Certainly no one of importance had a locker there.

Alice took Alan aside and fixed him closely with her deep, calm eyes.

"How long have we been friends?" she demanded.

"Uh-oh," he said, mock nervousness covering his nervousness. "What, are you breaking up with me?"

"No," she said. "Are *you* breaking up with *me?*"

"What the hell are you talking about?"

"Look," she said, speaking quickly in a jumble of pronouns and definite articles that might or might not have added up to English: "I know you have other friends and I have other friends and I know that I'm not interested in you *like that* and that you're not interested in me *like that* but I know and I think *you* know that when you *do* like somebody *like that* or if I liked somebody *like that* it might make it harder for us to be friends in the same way."

Alan stared at her blankly. "First of all, who said anything about liking anyone *that way?*" he asked finally. "And second of all, what does that have to do with you and me?"

"I'm just saying," she said, taking a deep breath. "I'm just saying that people grow up, and that I accept that."

"This is ridiculous," he said, standing up. "I don't even know why we're having this conversation."

"A long time ago," Alice went on patiently, "we used to say that when we grew up, we would live together forever and always be friends. I'm just saying that we both know now that that's not going to happen. One of these days there's going to be someone who matters to you more than me, and I just wanted to give you permission. I'm just saying."

"What *have* you been smoking?" he asked her angrily.

Alice waited for him to stop blustering. Then she said, "I just wanted to ask you one thing."

"What? Will I remember to write? Stop looking at me like you're going off to a convent!"

"I just want you to consider someone near you who likes you *that way*. I'm just saying if you wanted to go out with Agnes, I wouldn't object at all."

"Agnes?" He realized his mouth was gaping open, a serious breach of the rules of cool detachment. He shut it. *"Agnes?"* he said, again. *"Agnes* wants me to ask her out?"

Alice waited him out again; she was very good at that.

"I *can't* go out with Agnes," he explained to her. "Going out with Agnes would be like going out with you, only wor—" He stopped himself, not quite in time, and saw something in her eyes he'd never expected to see. A flicker of pain passed through them, and she turned away from him quietly and walked down the hall.

"Come on, Alice!" he called after her, but she didn't turn. A knot of sixth-grade girls broke apart to let her pass and giggled as they watched Alan watch Alice walk away.

It was Friday afternoon, and because of the stupid restriction, he wouldn't be able to talk to her until Monday. Who knew if by then she would be over it, or whether there would be a stupid festering cesspool of awkwardness between them. He raised his hands to the heavens and waited for an answer. One of the sixth graders giggled, and the full force of how stupid he looked fell upon Alan. He must look like his little old grandmother, the one who was always appealing to a hearing-impaired God.

Well, he understood her now. "*Oy vey*," he muttered to the heavens.

That night he lay on his bed in the dark, listening to the automated voice read off the passing seconds. The voice was still counting the minutes with robotic cheerfulness in his ear when he woke in the morning. Juliet had not called. Alan felt disgusting, dirty, as if he'd slept in his clothes. The memory of the stupid conversation with Alice kept playing in his mind. He cursed Keith for suggesting that Alice cared in the first place, and then he cursed his father for grounding him, and he cursed Alice for being an idiot, and then he cursed them all over again.

His father wasn't there when he got downstairs. Trish was scrambling eggs at the stove.

"Well, prisoner," she asked cheerfully. "What shall we do together all weekend? I am charged with keeping you from your friends, and as I suspect that you can have your homework done by noon today by the absolute latest, the weekend stretches before us as barren as the Sahara Desert. Let's go to Maine."

"I don't want to go to Maine."

"But I don't want to be stuck in this house trying to foil your little subterfuges. This restriction is growing old. Let's go to Maine."

"I don't like Maine. There are mice in the cabin."

"There *are* mice in the cabin. I will pack mousetraps. Let's go to Maine."

When she was like this, she got her way. And she was right; going away would meet the requirements of his restriction without having to remind him of it every three minutes. Besides, it would serve Juliet right to call and have the voice mail pick up.

It was a four-hour drive, and that, too, was a mercy. It ate up Saturday morning, and even if Trish did ask him awkward, prying questions, he could always fall asleep. When he woke up, they had innocuous conversations about the holidays. This was good: it suggested that the nonsense about moving back to Cincinnati was over.

When they reached the cabin, they went inside just long enough to turn on the heat and set the mousetraps; then they drove forty minutes to civilization and ate pizza and bought two lobsters to bring home and execute for dinner. Alan went for a walk in the woods when they got back to the cabin. There was something about the last oblivious hours of a lobster that always depressed him. They tasted good, though.

The cabin was on twenty acres of woods and meadow. Alan tramped through the pine trees, breathing in the clean and sticky smell of their sap. When he broke through into the meadow he was depressed to see how mangy and frostbitten it looked compared to the way it was in summer. The meadow was beautiful in the summer. In the summer you could go out in the twilight and sit on the big rock that lay at the edge of the wood and watch the deer come out of the trees to graze, silent as ghosts on their tiny hooves. Alan used to go there a lot. He liked watching the protective mothers standing over their fawns, pricking their ears at the slightest danger. There was something about them that made him all goopy and sentimental, and he always remembered them in the fall whenever he heard the crack of a shotgun.

There was a time when Alan had caused some unpleasantness around his father's hunting, but that would never happen again, not only because Alan had acquired a black belt in cool immunity, but also because all the shotguns were gone from the cabin. Trish had thrown them all away because Alan and Keith had shot each other.

It was boredom that had made them do it. There was simply nothing to do for two weeks in a cabin in the woods, especially when your aunt refused to teach you to drive. As the days dragged on, Alan and Keith had sat on the sagging couches and tried to watch the TV with its rotten reception. They had sat in other positions on the couches and tried to play poker with a maimed deck of cards. Finally, they lay down on the couches in a desperate attempt to be comfortable, and discussed the Meaning of Life.

"What's the point to all this living?" Alan had asked Keith, staring up at the cabin's ceiling. It wasn't a rhetorical question—he really wanted to know. Of all the things Alan saw no point to, life was prime among them.

"Why is everyone so damn sure life has a meaning?" Keith responded.

Strangely, Alan had never thought of that in terms that were quite so stark. He struggled to sit up.

"What do you mean?" he asked. "So there's no meaning, no lessons to be learned?"

"Just because there's no meaning, doesn't mean there's no lessons to be learned," Keith retorted. "Don't stick your hand in boiling oil, there's a lesson—but that doesn't mean there's any meaning to the universe."

"Huh," said Alan, collapsing back onto the sunken springs of the sofa. "You might be right."

They'd lain there a long time, contemplating the meaninglessness of the universe, and then Alan's eyes had caught the shotguns hanging on their pegs over the door. There was another instrument of meaninglessness, a metal tube that could dispatch a deer whose only crime was to be born with four legs—not for food, not for anything really, just a lark, just: "I think I'll cause some death today."

"Huh," he mused idly. "I wonder what it feels like, being shot."

"Want to find out?" That was Keith; always game, always insane. They'd talked it over as they searched in vain for a comfortable way to sit on the sagging couches, and finally, they'd taken all the phone books they could find, bound them around their middles with duct tape, loaded the shotgun with bird shot, and gone out to the deer meadow.

They'd stood pretty far away from each other, and Keith had raised the gun. Alan had stared at him across the wildflowers. For a moment, he felt a little sick and scared as he looked into the shotgun's dead black eyes. But his blood was cold, *sang-froid*, and his brain scientific; he would not back down from the experiment. He raised his hand to tell Keith he was ready. There was a crack, and Keith fell down from the kick of the gun. Alan didn't notice. He felt a sharp pain in one leg, and a great punch in the chest; he was on the ground before he knew it. Weakly, he raised one hand to tell Keith he was all right, but he didn't want to get up. He lay among the white Queen Anne's lace and the purple clover and stared up at the wispy clouds that drifted quickly through the sky. He almost felt he could feel the earth spinning.

The buzz of insects was loud in his ears as he wondered what would happen if the ground opened up and let him fall deep into the dirt. Would there be any record of his passing, back up on earth, or would he leave as few ripples on the surface as his mother had, when she had sunk out of his life?

W HEN THEY GOT BACK FROM MAINE on Sunday afternoon, there was a letter for Alan stuffed into the mailbox. He was pretty sure he recognized the dopey handwriting, and his heart was pounding as he skipped up the stairs to read it. It *was* a letter from Juliet, a long, rambling letter, asking him if he'd been kidnapped and urging him to call her; she apologized not once or twice but four times for falling asleep Friday night before she'd called him, and she enclosed an envelope she had found in the culvert on Saturday afternoon.

When he was done reading the letter, he laid it on his lap. His heart was beating curiously fast. He had never received a letter he had wanted to keep before. After his mother had died, he used to entertain vague fantasies that he would find a hidden letter that she had left for him, a letter she had left just in case she was suddenly swept off the face of the earth. In his fantasies, he kept that letter in the secret part of his desk drawer and took it out when times got hard. In the hard times after they'd bought the new house, when Trish had just arrived to beat off the screaming loneliness, he used to lie in bed and pretend that he'd found a letter like that.

Now he smoothed out the pages of Juliet's letter and read it over again. It practically glowed with the promise of her friendship, although when he looked carefully at the words, he couldn't find any explicit declaration of her affection. But it didn't matter. The real truth was *between* the words—poetry had taught him that. Real truth could only be seen out of the corner of the eye—looking for meaning directly was like looking at shadows by shining a flashlight on them. He put the note in his desk drawer and stood up. He knew what he needed to do.

Trish was sitting at the kitchen table, reading Saturday's paper. "Your father called," she said. "He and Cheryl had a sudden chance to go to some meeting in Aruba, so they'll be gone all week."

Alan shrugged. In truth he was relieved, but he didn't have time for complicated emotions. "Listen," he said, "I'm done with the restriction. I've learned my lesson and all that, and I want to go out."

She raised her eyebrow at him. "You've learned your lesson?" she repeated. "And what lesson would that be?"

Ah, that was a stumper. He could not even really remember what he had done, this time.

"Uh . . ." he temporized. "I shouldn't tell my father I wish he was dead?"

Trish nodded grimly and turned back to the paper.

"That might be a good idea. Fine, go out. If your father wants to go gallivanting about in the Caribbean, I'm not going to do his dirty work for him." Then she looked up again. There was a passing sad expression on her tired features. "I shouldn't have said that," she said. "It was unkind. Alan, has it ever occurred to you that your father might be a little bit frightened of you?"

"No," Alan answered. "It hasn't occurred to me, because it's insane." He went back into the hall and collected his cell phone from the place Trish always kept it during periods of confiscation. Then he grabbed his jacket and left the house.

"You're off restriction!" Juliet squealed when she answered the phone.

"Yeah—I charmed my way past the guards."

"Did you get what I left for you?"

"I got it"—huskily.

"So what do you think?"

Alan mumbled.

"You *liked* it?" Juliet repeated. "I would have thought that envelope would excite the spy in you more than *that*."

The envelope in her letter! He had completely forgotten about it. He turned back into the house and ran up the stairs to where he had let it drop to the floor. He snatched it up and looked at the name on it: Marc Portland. Marc—the lame Frenchy spelling marked it for interpretation. But how? What nefarious secrets were hidden in those dozen letters? A lesser spy might have given up, but Agent 666 was insightful, he was perceptive, and the brilliant engine that was his brain made him reverse the initial letters: Parc Mortland. And *Parc Mortland* was far from innocent nonsense. Take *mort*, for example. Wasn't that "death" in French? He was pretty sure it was, and certain that French was called for, what with the lame Frenchy spelling of Marc: Mortland, deathland, death to the land . . . and parc—hold on, hold your horses, could it be, *sacré bleu, mon dieu, sainte merde*, it was, PARC wasn't just a Frenchy word for a grassy place to lay down your beret but was, it really was, an anagram of CRAP.

CRAP: *death to the land*—it was a warning.

"You're kidding," said Juliet when she heard this analysis.

"I only wish I was. They're not going to stop with Murphy. They've tagged the new governor, for sure, and maybe that's not all."

"Then I call an emergency meeting, Secret Agent 666," Juliet announced. "Can you meet me in the culvert? I can be there in twenty minutes."

He was there in ten. He paced the bridge, waiting for her to come, breathing in deep lungfuls of the crisp autumn air, and feeling the great pleasure of being alive. Suddenly he turned in a quick circle, arms outstretched, face up to the brilliant sky, and then he stopped, blushing, hoping that no one had seen him in this *Sound of Music* moment. No one was there, except a moving speck. Then the moving speck moved closer and became Juliet, flying down the road like a vision on her bicycle, her scarf billowing out behind her. She rode right up to him, and the bike described a gorgeous arc around him as she came to a stop: the girl had flair.

"All right, 666," she said to him, stepping gracefully off the bike and fighting the wind to keep the scarf out of her face. "What about the rest of the envelope?"

They looked at it together:

MARC PORTLAND

1123 LEE ST.

LEXINGTON, MA 02473

"Lee Street . . ." murmured Alan, and then it all fell into place. Lee: who were the famous Lees of history? General Lee, of course—that hero of the Way Things Were, an apt hero for the conservative minds of CRAP. And who else, hold the phone—a chill settled upon Secret Agent 666. It was clear as day.

"Lee Harvey Oswald," he said. "The man who shot President Kennedy. They're promising death to the land—death to democracy, just like Mrs. Perry said—by pulling another LHO on Fordham."

"An LHO?"

For a moment he felt a flicker of disappointment that she didn't know what he'd meant—Alice would have known he'd meant a Lee Harvey Oswald right away—but nevertheless the admiration in Juliet's eyes was very gratifying.

"And Lexington's obvious, isn't it?" he went on. "'The Cradle of American Liberty'—and American Liberty's just like American Spirit, and that ties it to CRAP for sure. . . ." His voice trailed off. "And just think," he mused. "We're the only ones who know."

"Well, what do we do now?"

"Enmesh them in a web of evidence, of course."

"But where do we find it?"

"Anywhere. Everywhere." Alan waved his arm to encompass the culvert, the bridge, the trees, the sky, the brick police station, the American flag snapping in the gusty wind. "The world is our crime scene." And he explained to her how the SRU had interpreted license plates, missing letters on street signs, scraps of notes, Tampax packaging, newspapers, and radio ads. "Even here," he said, pointing to an overflowing trash can. Someone had thrown out a bottle of Murphy's Oil Soap there, and Alan seized it. "Obvious," he proclaimed. "They cleaned Murphy's clock and they're going to get Fordham, too."

"I had no idea there were clues everywhere," Juliet said.

"Oh yes," Alan assured her. "The world abounds with meaning."

All that afternoon, they scoured the culvert for clues. It was so easy with Juliet, and so fun. The blood rushed through his body as they ran from one side of the embankment to the other in response to imagined threats; he found himself taking huge gulpfuls of air as if he were a starving man wolfing down a meal. He felt a strange sensation in his chest, and finally identified it as contentment. For the first time in a long time, he felt simply happy. He let himself fall to the frosty ground, arms outstretched, and Juliet fell down beside him. Slowly, his hand reached out and felt for hers, and together, the two of them watched the carefree clouds chase one another around the sky.

His contentment was so complete it took him until the next morning to remember Alice and the stupid, dysfunctional conversation by her locker the Friday before. He probably wouldn't have remembered then, either, except that she was waiting for him at the big rock.

"I hear you're off restriction," she accused.

"Yeah—of course, my father might disagree when he comes back from Aruba."

"You didn't call me."

"Was I supposed to call you?"

"You *used* to call me when you got off restriction."

"I didn't have anything to say."

"You didn't *used* to need anything to say to call me," she reminded him. "Besides, we *do* have something to talk about."

"We do?"

She almost stamped her foot.

"What's *with* you, Alan?" she demanded. "Are we not friends anymore? Is this what happens, when you find someone new? I—"

"Oh, get off your high horse, Alice," he said. The bell was ringing. *Do not ask for whom the bell tolls, Alice, it tolls for homeroom.* "Look, I gotta go—"

But Alice ignored the bell. "Oh, am I on some high horse? I thought I was just worried about our relationship."

"Oh, *crap*," said Alan. "Our *relationship*? What are we, married?"

Some people might backpedal when they saw how much pain they were causing; some people, if they regretted their words, might try to take them back. But not Alan. He was angry at Alice, even if he didn't know why, and though he'd hurt her as surely as if he'd punched her in the stomach, he didn't really care. It wasn't until he saw the look in her eyes as he walked right past her at lunch that he realized with a pang that he was not so different from Rory Frankel after all. Walking by her like that, casting a look of disdain towards her—it was just like the way Rory Frankel smashed his fist into Kaufman's face, as if he could wipe off the miserable weakness he saw there by grinding it into a bloody pulp.

When the last bell rang, Alan avoided Keith and the others by hanging back to talk to Perry. That day she'd written out a poem by Emily Dickinson on the board, all about feeling like an outsider, and the words framed her now as she stood at her desk:

I'm nobody! Who are you?
Are you nobody, too?

Then there's a pair of us — don't tell!
They'd banish us, you know.

How dreary to be somebody!
How public, like a frog
To tell your name the livelong day
To an admiring bog!

"Nice poem, Perry," Alan said to her. "It was very sensitive of you to try to make us all feel better about ourselves through the magic of poetry. Now I see Rory Frankel is just a frog, and my self-esteem's gone through the roof."

"It's not very subtle, is it?" she laughed, looking at the words.

"Not so you'd notice."

"Still, it's an important sentiment."

Alan shrugged. "I'm sure it will be a consolation to Kaufman, next time the frogs beat the crap out of him."

"Who's Kaufman?" she asked, wrinkling her brow. He liked that about her. She was so stuck in her poetry that she knew right away what he'd meant about the frogs, but she didn't even know who Kaufman was. Well, it was a big school; he didn't really want to get into it.

"Nobody," he answered. "Well, thanks for the uplift and all—see you tomorrow."

Mrs. Perry rolled her eyes. *"Au revoir, enfant terrible,"* she said. "I'll try to dig up something suitable for your sophisticated palate tomorrow. A little E. E. Cummings, perhaps: 'Humanity/i hate you'?"

"Sounds good," he said, and he went off to find Juliet.

She was leaning against his locker—*his*, though hers was right near it, close enough to lean on—and tapping pointedly at the face of her watch.

"I should think what with all that listening to the time, you'd have a better sense of it," she scolded him.

What an opening—referring like that to the secret phone calls they'd shared at the most intimate time of night! He grinned wider, uncontrollably. It was not the mask of cool, but there was no helping that anymore.

"Sorry. I had to talk to Perry."

"Shall we go?" She proffered her slender arm, and he bowed before laying his fingertips on the frayed nylon of her parka. She was very tall, but he didn't care. He walked out of the school surrounded by her clean smell, and he didn't care who saw them as they walked off to the culvert.

It was a glorious afternoon: the blue sky at its bluest, the white clouds at their cottoniest, and Juliet racing up to him holding a scrap of paper for his perusal, her pink scarf flying out behind her. It was an American Spirit cigarette package ripped so only ERICA SPI was left. This was irrefutably a message from CRAP—a defiant message that CRAP knew the SRU was on the Erica Fordham case. It was also, incontrovertibly, an insult.

"Do you see what they're saying?" Alan demanded.

"What?"

"They're saying they know we're onto them, and they don't care. They're as good as saying they see us watching

them and they're not scared. 'Go off and play, little girls.'
That's what they're saying with this."

"The gall of them," Juliet agreed. "Well, we'll show
them, won't we, Secret Agent 666?"

"We certainly will, Agent 4X35. It's probably a good
thing. To underestimate your enemy is to arm him."

"Where did you read that, a fortune cookie?"

"You watch, Juliet. This is where our disguises as four-
teen-year-olds will lure them to their destruction."

"Yeah," she said happily. "We'll get 'em."

He felt that he had never been happier than in the week
that followed. He and Juliet looked for clues and found
them everywhere. For example, there might be a tiny
piece of graffiti scratched into a park bench: XY. As Alan
mused, the possibilities expanded. It might be a simple
wheel code, where you start some random place in the
alphabet, say G for A. Then H would be B; I, C, and so
forth. There are not many words in the English language
made up of two consecutive letters, which meant (if XY
were indeed that sort of code), that the message might be
as cryptic as HI or perhaps, more meaningfully, NO. Or it
might stand for EF—the governor's initials. And from E to
X there were nineteen letters—the number nineteen
must somehow be significant. And *why* was CRAP so bent
on destroying Erica Fordham? Or did XY refer to the
chromosomes of a man, to male domination? Or was it
the second half of Juliet's secret-agent name: SEXY, like
they were threatening to cut Juliet in half? Most likely, it
was all of these things: CRAP was very crafty indeed.

It amazed Alan in those days how easy it was to talk to Juliet, and how easy it was to be quiet. He had always hated silence before; it always sounded to his ears like a joke falling flat. There were always those moments in the jumbled mosaic of conversation with his friends when everyone fell silent all at once, and they would look around the room, tongue-tied and uncomfortable. "Eighteen past the hour," his mother used to say. He never found out where she had acquired that particular catchphrase, but she used it every time sudden silence fell over the room. Eighteen past the hour: Alan's least favorite time of day. He remembered the few months after his mother had been killed, when it seemed that all the clocks in the house had been stuck at eighteen past; the house had been filled with a horrible, crushing silence that weighed down on him like some sort of medieval torture. But with Juliet, silence was a golden thing, a thing of intimacy and comfort.

One Wednesday afternoon, as they lay in the culvert, belly down, commando style, Alan realized they had not said anything for nearly ten minutes. In that intimate silence, that comfortable silence, Alan slid over his hand and took Juliet's. They lay there, holding hands, not looking at each other, and Alan closed his eyes. He smiled. He felt as if he were extending out little suckers that were taking root in their shared silence. His life was entwining with hers. He felt the pulse of her hand, and it was the same as his own.

Juliet sat up then. Delicately, she extracted her hand from his and blew on her fingers.

"You know what I was thinking?" she said.

He knew what he wished she was thinking, but apparently it wasn't it.

"Have you noticed that assassins always have three names? John *Wilkes* Booth. James *Earl* Ray. Lee *Harvey* Oswald. Does that mean something?"

"Yeah," Alan answered. "Make middle names illegal."

Juliet laughed. When she laughed like that, her top lip pulled back and showed her crooked left canine.

"Do you have a middle name?" he asked her.

"Jennifer, if you can believe it."

"Juliet Jennifer Jones, huh?" It felt good on his tongue; and it was another thing to bind them together, that he knew her middle name.

"And you?"

"Alan. Alan *is* my middle name. My first name's Charles, but you're not allowed to tell anyone that."

"Can't *I* call you Charles? I like the idea that I have a secret name for you."

Alan considered. He had always hated the name Charles—it was all he needed for Rory Frankel to start calling him Chuck (upchuck, chuck wagon). But on the other hand, it sounded different when it came out of Juliet's mouth. He shrugged.

"Well then, I will," she said, standing up. "Ugh. I better go home and practice. It's very hard, this having two careers."

"I'll walk you home," Alan offered quickly.

"Don't bother," she said. "I'll see you in the morning."

He hated it when she went. There was a word for it: *deflated*. That pretty much described it perfectly. He sat there alone, deflating, weighing the "I like the idea that I have a secret name for you" against the "Don't bother," and he interpreted the nuances of her silence. Their time together was full of clues, and Secret Agent 666 stood there, trying to figure out exactly what they meant.

Then she was back, leaning over the edge of the bridge.

"Hey, Charles!"

"Yeah?"

"Call me if the Boss shows up, all right?"

"Of course!" he told her, and then she was gone.

She had come back, she had called him Charles—these clues, too, meant something, though Secret Agent Alan Green could never be sure what.

There was a message from Alice to call her when he got home, but Alan ignored it. Instead he swaggered around the kitchen looking for a snack, taking a swig of orange juice right from the carton, and generally strutting around like a bantam cock, though no one was there to see it. Finally, he picked up the phone and called her.

"Alan," she said, in a strangely dead voice. "Well! I didn't think *you'd* call me back. I didn't think you remembered me."

He rolled his eyes. It was just like that "knock knock" joke they used to tell:

Will you remember me in twenty years?

Of course.

Will you remember me in fifty years?

Of course.

Knock knock.

Who's there?

It's Alice. YOU FORGOT ME! Oh—he just got it; he was supposed to say "Alice who?" and *then* she was supposed to say "You forgot me!" They'd always done that wrong. No wonder it had never been funny.

"Well, I'm calling you back," he said now.

"So what have you been doing?"

What was this, the third degree? He tried to keep it breezy. "Oh, you know, the usual—saving humanity from the depredations of CRAP, that sort of thing."

"You *have?*" she accused him. "You're playing the SRU without me?"

"Well," he told her, "it's not so much without you as *with* Juliet."

There was a long silence.

"Are you trying to tell me something?" she said at last.

"Not particularly," he answered. "Is there something I should be trying to tell you?"

"Oh, forget it," she said, and hung up.

A little while later, the phone rang again. Alan jumped on it, but it wasn't Juliet. It was Agnes.

That was strange. Agnes did not usually call him; in fact, Agnes usually froze if they were ever alone. Her usual mode of behavior was to stand three steps behind Alan and moon at him with her big sad eyes. Once Alan's father had made some snide comment and paraphrased from Shakespeare: "I am your spaniel; and Alan, the more you beat me, I will fawn on you. . . ." Alice had leaped to Agnes's defense, like a mother lion with a threatened cub. She was always fiery when Agnes was attacked. It was kind of sweet, in a way—at least, he used to think so.

Now here was Agnes the spaniel, calling him out of the blue. He flicked on the TV—if you didn't have something else to do when talking to Agnes, she would drive you nuts.

"So what's up?" he asked, flipping through the channels.

"Fine," said Agnes. That was just like her, never answering the right way. She was stupid with slang. He remembered one year when he'd gone to a concert in the city with Keith and his dad, and when Agnes asked how it was, he'd told her it was *sick*.

"Why?" she'd asked. "What was wrong with it?"

"*Sick*, Agnes," he'd tried to explain. "*Sick*, like it was good."

"Why didn't you say it was good, then?"

"Because it was better than good—it was *sick*." Then he'd told her to forget it.

Now she repeated herself. "I'm fine," she said. "How are you?"

"Fine."

"What's up?"

"What's up? You're the one who called me."

"Yes, I did."

"And, why . . . ?" he prompted.

"I called to see how you were."

"Well, mission accomplished: I'm fine." Ah: monster trucks. *This* he could watch.

"I'm also calling about Alice."

"About Alice? Is she still totally pissed at me?"

"She's not *mad*," Agnes said primly, as if unconsciously correcting his language. "She's *hurt*."

"Oh, come on," Alan interrupted. "She's not hurt, she's pissed! What gives her the right to be pissed at me?"

"I don't think you need a right to be mad at someone," Agnes mumbled.

But Alan had warmed to his subject. Righteous anger at Alice surged through his veins. "Well, I don't see what the hell *she* has to be mad at! What the hell did I even do to her?"

"She's not mad because you *did* something," Agnes said. "She's hurt because you *didn't* do something. She's hurt because—" Here's where it would start, the sputtering and the not finishing of sentences. He rolled his eyes again.

"Because of what?"

"Because she feels betrayed."

"Betrayed! That's an awfully big word, don't you think? What heinous treachery have I done now?"

"You kicked her out of the SRU."

"I didn't kick her out!"

"But you want to, and that's the same thing."

The natural response to a truthful accusation was anger. "Well, she's not the only one who's mad! She's been riding me for *weeks!* Why does she think she can insult me and still expect me to—"

"When did she insult you?" cried Agnes. "When did she do anything to hurt you?"

"She said I couldn't be trusted with a baby!"

"Oh, Alan," Agnes sighed. "That was weeks ago, and she was joking—teasing you, like she always does, because she likes you and because you're her best friend."

"Oh, Jesus Christ in a horse barn," Alan sputtered. "That's not what a friend does. I have other friends who don't insult me. *Juliet* doesn't insult me. It's a hell of a lot more fun hanging out with people like that."

"And that's what makes Alice sad," Agnes explained patiently. "She's sad that you like Juliet instead of liking her."

"This is ridiculous," he said. "I gotta go." He hung up.

He stood for a minute, looking at the phone, and then he picked it up again and dialed.

"Well, now, stranger, I didn't expect to hear from *you*," drawled Keith.

"Why not?" said Alan, peeved. "Gone deaf since I saw you last?"

"I could've, for all you'd know. Where've you been?"

"In the culvert . . . with Juliet." (This, a little less subtly than he'd planned.)

"I heard. Alice called me."

"Was she all weird with you, too? I don't know what her problem is. She gets more like a girl every day."

"She kinda *is* a girl, though," Keith pointed out.

"I *know* she's a girl, dodo," said Alan. "I mean, she didn't used to *act* like one."

Keith sighed lugubriously. "I haven't exactly noticed you mind people who act like girls," he said.

"I mind when it's *Alice*," Alan pronounced. "Alice should just be like Alice and not like, well, Agnes."

The whole conversation was putting him in a bad mood.

"Want to hang out tomorrow?" Keith offered.

"Sure, why not?"

"You sure you don't have other plans?"

"She dances on Thursdays."

Keith sighed, and then he began to sing, in a low, mournful tone, "'Let me be your rag doll, until your china comes. . . .'"

"What's that all about?"

"Just a sonata for a second fiddle," said Keith in mock-mournful tones. "What, I only get Juliet's scraps? *This* is why Alice is pissed off, you know."

"Jesus Christ," Alan answered. "I'll see you in the morning."

When Trish came in to call him for dinner, Alan was in a better mood. He'd gone to get the video games out of his father's closet and was happily sitting on the floor destroying hordes of his enemies. He was in such a good mood he even initiated conversation by repeating what Juliet had said about the three names of assassins.

"While your analysis is credible," Trish said, "I suspect the use of the middle name has more to do with not wanting to confuse the dastardly criminals with other law-abiding citizens cursed with the name John Thaddeus Booth, Lee Algernon Oswald, or James Habbekuk Ray. You'll notice Leon Czolgosz, who assassinated President McKinley, never goes by his middle name."

"Czglogogloz?" he repeated.

"Czglozoglozoglogz," she confirmed. They laughed together. Only the sighing sound of the front door opening interrupted them.

"I guess your father's home," Trish said, getting up from the table to welcome him. Quickly, Alan put his plate in the sink. He felt slightly sick as he hurried up the back staircase into his room. Picking up the joystick, he flicked on the TV and turned up the volume. You might as well face the enemy with an Uzi in your hands; it's as good a way as any other.

He heard his father's footsteps down the hall and the creak of the door. Alan went on playing. It was strange, listening to his father standing there, breathing. They had not really talked since the moment they had fought under the streetlight. It seemed like a lifetime away. And now his father was standing there, with his fakey Aruba tan, and Alan realized he didn't have anything more to say.

"Turn off the game, Alan," said his father sharply. "I want you to come down and talk to Cheryl."

This was so shocking that Alan dropped the joystick. "*Cheryl?*" he sputtered. "Why is Cheryl here? I thought you promised I wouldn't have to—"

"Have you completely forgotten our conversation?" his father snapped, throwing his hands into the air.

"I don't *think* so," said Alan, playing for time.

"Well then, perhaps you will recall that Cheryl and I are getting *married*. All this . . . this *charade* of yours, this childish pretense that you are incapable of being in the same room with her—it has got to stop. *Now*."

But Alan had recovered. "Sure thing, Pop," he said, picking up the joystick again. "No problem." On the screen, his overly muscled alter ego laid down his gun and did not pick up another weapon. He stood still for an animated second, shuddered with the impact of the bullets, wavered, and fell. Alan wiped his hands on his pants and stood up. If Keith had been there, he would have understood. He would have jumped to his feet and given Alan a standing ovation, shouting "Oscar clip! Oscar clip!" Because that's what this was: Alan's big scene, the scene to show his emotional depth. But really, there was no emotional depth inside him—he felt nothing but weariness. He couldn't even really summon up anger towards Cheryl. It *was* a charade, to some degree—but to give up the charade is to acknowledge defeat. The troops must be marshaled; the battle would go on.

"Let's go, then," he said in a ridiculously cheerful voice.

"I mean it, Alan. You are to show Cheryl the respect she deserves as a woman, as my fiancée, and as a guest in this house."

"The respect she deserves. Gotcha."

His father grabbed him roughly by the shoulders and spoke in a low, hard voice. "If you think this dummkopf behavior of yours is going to impress me, think again." His fierce eyes tried to hold Alan's face still as surely as his hands grasped Alan's arm, and Alan suddenly felt deflated for the second time that day. All of the sympathetic conversations he had planned to have with Cheryl about the bad reputation of stepmothers seemed irrelevant now. What did it matter if Cheryl moved in or not? If truth be told, he felt, the worst thing about her moving in was that she would bring her new husband with her.

T HE NEXT DAY AT SCHOOL it was clear that the Parker twins had decided to avoid him. Alice walked right by him with her head held high; Agnes, like a sadder shadow of a spaniel, followed behind and watched after Alan with her sorrowful puppy-dog eyes.

At first, Keith treated it like a joke.

"Stop fighting!" he screamed as Alan turned away from Alice in the halls at the end of the day. "I can't stand it! I've already been through one divorce, and I can't go through another. *It's the always the children who get caught in the middle!*"

"You wouldn't be caught in the middle if you agreed she's acting like a royal bitch," Alan said. "Hey, can you wait here? I want to go say good-bye to Juliet."

"I'll still be waiting here in the chopped-liver section," Keith whined.

Alan gave him half a vague "whatever" gesture and ran

back to where Juliet was getting her shoe bag out of her locker.

"Have a good class," he told her.

"I will."

"Remember CRAP could be infiltrating even there," Alan warned. "Don't let your guard down, just because you're in a leotard."

"I never do," she said.

"I mean, they could be anywhere," Alan went on. This was totally lame, but his brain was not functioning at peak efficiency—sometimes she had that effect on him.

"I know, I know," she said. "But I really have to go now."

"God, you're whipped," Keith observed when Juliet walked off.

"Am not," said Alan automatically. "It's just I like being with her. And . . . she's a good spy."

"Oh Lord!" Keith pleaded. "Tell me you're not boring her to death with that stupid game."

Alan felt a flash of annoyance. "It's not stupid," he said. And then: "We did predict that first assassination, didn't we? We said something would happen, and that was the afternoon they assassinated her."

Keith started to say something, but changed his mind and laughed.

"What's so funny?" Alan demanded.

"Assassinate."

"What's funny about that?"

"What's not funny about a word that starts off with two

asses? Come on. Let's go to the Center. I want to get a burger."

"A burger!" Alan exclaimed, looking at his watch. "You do know, don't you, that normal people eat burgers at mealtimes. What are you going to eat for dinner if you eat burgers for snacks?"

"Two burgers," Keith answered good-naturedly. "You coming?"

They went down to the Center and sat at a greasy table in the back of the sub shop.

"So," said Keith, taking an enormous bite out of his burger, "when are you going to make your move on Ballerina Juliet?"

"I'm not making any move."

"Why not?"

"Jesus, Keith! We're just friends, all right?"

"You know you're never going to be more than friends if you keep playing that stupid game, don't you?"

"Who said I want to be more than friends? Besides, it's not stupid."

"Yeah, I know. It's very *mature*, playing James Bond in a concrete tunnel."

Alan could not contain his irritation. "Well, it's a hell of a lot more fun than sitting on my fat ass playing video games!"

"You used to like video games," Keith commented. "Anyway, I'm not playing them too much, either. I've been practicing for an audition."

"Audition?" Alan laughed. "For what? The Mr. Universe Pageant? I can't wait to see the bathing-suit competition!"

Keith put down his hamburger. "It's for a musical, if you must know," he said, sniffing in an offended sort of way. "*Carousel*."

"*Carousel?*" Alan repeated blankly. "That musical about the circus? What, they want you to be one of the elephants?" He laughed then, a little too loudly. There was something strange about the way the laugh sounded in his ears, and then he realized it was because he was laughing alone. Keith was staring at him, offended, and Alan's laughter died away.

"Alice is right about you, you know," said Keith after a long moment. "You really are turning into a bastard."

Alan stared. "I'm not turning into anything," he sputtered. A rising dread began tightening in his middle. What had happened? They had been joking around, and suddenly Keith was looking at him as if he wanted to punch him in the nose. "We always joke, remember? What's the matter with you, anyway?"

Keith stood up. "So maybe you're not changing," he said, putting down his burger. "Maybe you were always a bastard."

He walked out of the sub shop, leaving the remains of his snack on the plate. Alan sat there, sullenly nursing his Coke. *Fine*, he said in his head. *Go, if you're so damn sensitive. It wasn't like I harpooned you or anything.*

He walked home, wondering what to do. It seemed like a call to patch things up was in order. Alan would apologize, or at least give Keith a chance to say he was sorry. Because what had Alan done, anyway, that was so offensive? He'd been joking around, just like they always did, and Keith should realize he'd been acting like a jerk. But Keith wouldn't come to the phone.

"Tell him I'm not home," Alan heard him say to his mother.

"Tell him I can hear him!" Alan shouted.

"Tell him good!" Keith hollered back. "Maybe then he'll catch a hint."

"Forget it," said Alan, and he hung up. What the hell was wrong with Keith and Alice anyway? It was like he was standing still in the middle of a storm and everyone else was being blown away by some strange and savage wind. He didn't get it at all.

Friday afternoon it was freezing cold—nasty November cold. Alan and Juliet huddled next to the school out of the biting wind. Juliet blew on her gloved fingers as she watched Kaufman's mother leading him across the parking lot.

"He got totally jumped on the way home again yesterday," she said. "He told me about it at lunch."

Alan made a noncommittal noise. He was looking at the shape of Juliet's ear where it peeped out from beneath her hat; it was tiny and perfectly formed, like a little shell.

"It just makes me sick," said Juliet. "I went and told

Kellerman he should do something about it. I told him he should be ashamed not to. You know what he said? He said they can't do anything about rumors of things that happen outside of school. He said Morris hadn't complained, and then he made it sound like it was none of my business. Can you believe it?"

It was very small, that shell, small and perfect. Her hands, too, were tiny for someone so tall. What was that E. E. Cummings poem Perry had read to them—*nobody, not even the rain, has such small hands*. What the hell did that mean, anyway?

"Well, what do you think? Don't you think it's my business—all of our business?"

"Sure," mumbled Alan.

Juliet watched until Kaufman made it safely into his car, and then she turned away.

"Sometimes I feel totally responsible for him," she said.

She leaned against the rough concrete wall, and Alan leaned back beside her. She huddled against him, as if to steal his warmth, and that, along with other tucked-away evidence, made him bold. He stretched out his arm, not to put it around her or anything, just to stretch it—but his sleeve caught on the concrete on the way and tore a big gash in the soft Italian leather.

"Oh, oh!" Juliet cried. "Your beautiful jacket!"

"Don't worry about it," said Alan, suddenly embarrassed. "I'll get a new one. Come on—let's get to the culvert."

They walked over to the culvert in silence. To Alan, the

warm, comforting quiet felt like a thousand conversations passing between them. The words of that Cummings poem said it best: *your slightest look easily will unclose me/though i have closed myself as fingers, . . . /nobody, not even the rain, has such small hands.* It was a good poem. And because he was thinking about the poem, and wondering what it meant about the rain and its hands, it was Juliet, and not Alan, who saw them first.

"Charles!" she squealed. "It's them! It's the car!"

It was—it was the white Ford Probe with the CPR 1 plate, and it was driving past the police station towards the culvert. They began running as soon as it was out of sight, but the car was gone by the time they reached the bridge.

"That really was it, though," said Juliet. "The Boss's car."

"You know what we should do," Alan said, struck by inspiration. "A stakeout. We should stay here all night."

"We should!" she said, and then: "—but not tonight. I have to get home kinda early."

"Why?" Alan demanded. "What could possibly be more important than a stakeout with me to protect Democracy as we know it?"

"I need to practice. And besides, my parents are having some friends over for dinner, and I'm supposed to be friendly to their kid."

"Let me guess," said Alan, rolling his eyes. "It's Rory Frankel, and you're going to fall madly in love with him."

"Give me a break, Charles!" she said, hitting him on the

arm and almost sending him careening down the embankment. (And every touch, even the roughest, was stowed inside for him to interpret later.) "It's just some high school kid. All I know about him is that he's very tall."

"A mutant, eh? Maybe I should come, and make sure he doesn't push you around."

"Yeah, right," she said, skittering down into the culvert. "My hero."

"What do you mean by that?" Alan called down to her. But Juliet ignored him.

"Jeez!" she said, leaping from foot to foot. "It's freezing. Get down here and warm me up."

Get down here and warm me up. This time, it wasn't just the tone—it was the words, too. *Get down here and warm me up.* This was a declaration. First there was the familiarity implied in the imperative form of *get down here*, and then there was the *warm me up*—you wouldn't say *that* to Morris Kaufman. He hurried down the embankment and knelt in front of her, tucking her hands into her sleeves and drawing her feet under his legs to warm them. At last he put his arm awkwardly around her. They sat like that, not talking, for a long time, as the unspoken conversations flowed between them: *your slightest look easily will unclose me/though i have closed myself as fingers . . . /nobody, not even the rain, has such small hands.*

"Am I making your feet fall asleep?" he asked her suddenly.

"Yeah—but I don't mind."

"How can you not mind? Don't you hate it when your feet fall asleep?"

"I hate it if *I'm* the one making them fall asleep. I don't mind it when *you're* doing it, Charles."

Above the culvert, the skies parted; a ray of sunlight fell on Alan's face. At that moment, it seemed that all the angels were coming out of heaven and dancing around his head. From their long trumpets came a joyful clarion call: *alleluia, alleluia, alleluia.*

SATURDAY JULIET HAD TWO BALLET CLASSES. Alan sat in the house, oppressed by the grinding boredom. Finally, he threw on his coat and went out to the culvert. But it was boring and cold there without Juliet; he went home and watched TV as he waited for her to call.

"They didn't show up," he informed her when she finally phoned.

"Well, how long did you wait?"

"Twenty minutes?" Alan estimated generously.

"What kind of spy are you, anyway?" Juliet chided him. "What did you do then—play video games?"

"Maybe," Alan hedged.

He could hear the disapproval in her silence. "Don't you ever wish you had a calling—something you really wanted to do with your life?"

"Maybe video games *are* my calling," he suggested. "What's so wrong with that? What do you think I should do, join the ballet corps?"

"Corpse? It's pronounced ballet *core*, you know, and you wouldn't last *two minutes* in it. I know—come over—I'll show you."

"Come over?" he repeated. "Like, to your house?"

"*Yes*," she laughed. "*Yes*, like to my house."

He had not been to her house before. His spy senses were tingling as he crossed her threshold—it was clear from the reigning silence and the lack of cars in the driveway that they were alone. He smiled nervously.

"What do you want to do?"

"Show you that you wouldn't last five seconds in the ballet corps. Here—copy me—do this." Gamely he tried to imitate her movements, but three minutes later he fell wheezing to the floor, grabbing his sore thighs. Then she was kneeling beside him, undoing the laces of his sneakers. She slipped his shoes off his feet and he knew he would have fallen had he not already been on the floor. She ran her long finger down his sole, criticizing his instep; he thought he was going to die. Then she ran to her room and flew back with her toe shoes, the pink ties streaming out behind them. She knelt beside him again, pushing his jeans up his shins, and she put the toe shoes on his feet.

"What are you doing?"

"Showing you what it feels like."

It was indescribable, what it felt like. The satin of the shoe squeezing his foot, bending his toes; Juliet's hands warm on his shins as she crisscrossed the smooth satin ribbons on his legs; her head bent over his knees—he breathed more quickly.

"Okay," she said. "Up you go."

He stood, holding on to her arm.

"No—all the way up. *En pointe*. Up on your toes."

Tentatively, he put the box of the left shoe flat on the ground and tried to put his weight on it; for a moment, it was bearable.

"All the way up, big guy," Juliet laughed. He tried it—it was agonizing. He fell to the floor, nursing his toes.

"Jesus Christ," he panted. "How the hell do you do that? *Why* the hell do you do that?"

Juliet laughed. She was untying the shoes now and placing them on her own feet. Her hands were deft and sure as she whipped the ribbons around her beautiful ankles, and the pink of the ribbons on the brown of her skin was unbearably lovely. Then she lifted herself up elegantly and rose up on her toes. Impossibly, she raised one leg to the side, bent her knee, and pirouetted triumphantly on her pointed toe. Alan gaped.

"Doesn't that kill?"

"Yeah." She pulled off one shoe and showed him her feet: a mass of blisters and bunions. His heart hurt in his chest to see them, so sad and mutilated, compared with the perfect rest of her. "*Why* do you do it, then?" he asked.

Juliet shook her head. "I knew you wouldn't understand," she said haughtily. "I do it because it's worth it. I love it. And it's important."

"Important, how?"

"Art is important," she sniffed. "Beauty is important."

For a moment he knew she was right—not just from the

force of her conviction but from the painful longing she
had awakened in his heart by dancing so beautifully. He
fell back against the couch. Juliet sank down next to him,
untying the long ribbons from her ankles.

"Hey, Charles, can I ask you a personal question?" she
said, head bent over the toe shoes. "What was it like,
when your mother died?"

You'd think he'd have an answer all prepared for this
one; you'd think someone would have asked him this
before. But then again, most of his friends had known him
then, back in those strange, black days after she'd died,
back when he'd broken the window with his bare fist and
laughed inappropriately at her funeral.

"I don't know," he said.

"What do you mean, you don't know?"

"I haven't thought about it."

"I wasn't asking you what you *thought*, Alan. I was asking you what you *felt*. That's just what I'm always saying—you don't let yourself *feel* anything."

"I feel," he said defensively.

"Well, what was it like, then, when your mother died?"

"Well," he answered slowly, "when you were a little kid,
did you ever worry that your mother was going to die?
Wake up in the night and think about it?"

"I had nightmares about it, sometimes. A dream where
I was looking all over the house for her, and couldn't find
her."

"Well, that was what it felt like."

A long pause.

"Can I say something else?"

"Sure."

"I'm sorry I said that, about your not feeling anything."

"I feel a lot," he said. Then, more huskily: "I feel a lot for you."

She inched away from him, delicately, and Alan blushed furiously. But that night in bed, he replayed the afternoon with her as if it were a special USO entertainment for the soldiers of his resolve. He let himself remember the moment she had slipped the shoes over his feet, and the troops went mad over the memory of it.

She was certainly wrong about it: he did feel a lot. In the morning he felt he could not bear to go a whole day without seeing her. Little fragments of memory kept slipping before his eyes—the shoes, the *I don't mind it when you do it, Charles* day. He called her as soon as it seemed civilized. She agreed to meet him at the culvert, but not until three; it was an eternity until then.

It was freezing when she showed up. They shrank inside their coats and sat on their tingling fingers to keep them warm.

"Are they going to come soon?" Juliet asked for the eighth time. "I'm totally freezing." She crept out of the culvert and began to do a wild dance, the tarantella, the dance you were compelled to do when you were bitten by a tarantula.

"Come back," Alan pleaded. "If you're out there, the Boss will see you when he comes."

"Don't worry—I move fast."

She did a few more wild steps; she was beautiful.

"I could warm you up again," he suggested.

"Nah—if I sit down, I'll turn into a positive block of *ice*."

Alan came out of the culvert and lay down on the grass. *Lie down,* he told her in his head, and because they could speak without speaking, she did. They lay there a long time, and Alan wondered how it was that just being, just lying still without speaking, could seem so meaningful. Then Juliet sat up.

"We've been here for forty minutes, you know," she announced. "They're not coming."

"Sure they're coming," said Alan quickly. "We just have to be more patient."

"They didn't come yesterday and they're not coming today. I have to go home and practice."

"Aw, come on, Jules!" he protested. "Just a little longer."

She sat down again.

"All right—for *you*." Out of the corner of his eye he could see she was doing little foot exercises; he had lost her attention. He hated that. He wished she'd lie down again; he liked the warmth of her long length next to him. Suddenly he imagined dancing with her—slow dancing, like he'd done once with Marina Fotis in sixth grade; he thought of the stupid under-the-sea-themed school-sponsored dances he and Alice and Keith had always made fun of, and wished he could be there with Juliet.

"So, are you going, next Friday?"

"Next Friday?"

"You know—to the dance."

"To the *dance?*" She stared at him. "Do I seem that lame?"

"Well, you dance, don't you? It could be fun."

"Sure, I *dance*, but not with those morons. Listen, how much longer do I have to stay? I really have to practice. I only did twenty minutes this morning because we had this stupid brunch thing with some friends of my mother's."

"Ten minutes. I promise. Ten minutes and then I'll let you go. And you don't have to practice so much, do you, if you're so good?"

"*Yes*, I have to practice if I'm so good. And I'm probably so good *because* I practice. And besides, I *want* to practice. But you wouldn't understand that."

This was true; but he was beginning to wish it weren't. "I can't imagine wanting to do the same thing over and over, like that," he admitted honestly. "I can't imagine anything that I'd like to do that much." Actually, that wasn't so honest. There were plenty of things he'd like to do every day, and all of them involved Juliet.

"We've already been over this. It's because you don't have a calling. That's what dance is for me, a calling—it's something I *have* to do. I couldn't *not* do it. But you're not like that. Like today—if I go home, you won't stay and see if they show up—you'll go home instead."

Alan shrugged. "It's just more fun when you're here, that's all."

"But what about Fordham? Don't you need to stay here and protect her? Or are you going to admit it's just a game?"

"It's not a game!" he objected. Suddenly his voice was muffled; she had laid her soft hand over his mouth. The movement was so sudden and so intimate that for a moment he didn't notice that she was pointing up to the road above the culvert.

The white Ford Probe was back. It parked just off the bridge, and the door creaked open. Just on cue, the heavy footsteps of the Henchman came shuffling up the road.

Alan and Juliet scrambled back under the culvert, hardly daring to breathe. Up above, the Boss dragged on his cigarette, coughed, and cleared his throat. Twelve feet below, Alan and Juliet waited. Her eyes were full of mischief and fun. Slowly she fed her hand into Alan's and squeezed. Then the Boss began to speak, and Juliet's hand went slack in Alan's grasp.

"How many times are you going to screw this up, Lenny?"

The menace in his voice was so real that it suddenly stopped feeling at all like a game. Alan felt sick.

"Better to do it right than not be able to do it at all," Lenny mumbled.

"But you *aren't* doing it at all, are you? That's my point."

"I told you, I didn't have enough time. It needs to be perfect, or . . ." His voice trailed off as a troop of footsteps came tramping up the road. Laughter, giggles, the sound of a skateboard with one wiggly wheel, and then they were gone. Lenny went on.

"I *am* gonna do it—you know I'm gonna."

"Sure, Lenny," said the Boss, "but what I'm asking is *when*."

"On the twenty-third. I can get it done on the twenty-third."

"All right, then—on the twenty-third. But if it's *not* done then, Lenny, then you are. Done. You know what I mean. The twenty-third." A last drag on the cigarette, and then the butt came flying down. Feet crunched on the gravel, and then the white Ford Probe was gone. Lenny stood alone on the bridge, shuffling his feet in the gravel. Then he got into own his car and drove away.

"Oh my God."

"I know," breathed Juliet. "Did you hear them?"

He had heard them. Now he was quite sure something bad was happening. It was not a game anymore, and it was not fun.

"Should we . . ." he started, "you know, go to the police?"

"The police? Why?"

"Why?" he repeated stupidly. "Didn't you hear them?"

"Alan . . ."

"You're right," he answered. "No one would believe us. They're too clever." Then he had an idea. "You know what we could do," he said slowly. "We could write it up, just like it happened. So other people would see we knew it was a joke, before it got serious . . ."

"Sure," she said, more easily now. "That's a good idea."

So they went back to Alan's house and turned on his computer, and they began to write. They worked side by side, Alan at the computer, Juliet sometimes standing with her hand on Alan's dresser, using it as a barre, sometimes standing with her hand on his shoulder as he typed away. It took so long that Alan asked Trish if Juliet could stay for dinner; then they wrote steadily for another hour. Again and again, as Alan paused to think of the right words, it seemed ridiculous to him that Erica Fordham's life should be in danger while he, Alan, was sitting there so comfortably, his skin tingling under the pressure of Juliet's hand. He leaned back a little in the chair, and his head brushed the taut firmness of her stomach. He looked up and saw her smiling down at him; she put out her hand and ruffled his hair. A buzzer went off.

"What was that?"

"The intercom. It's dinnertime." He waved his hand towards the wall.

"You have an *intercom?*"

"Yeah—for servants, you know. Not that *we* have servants," he amended quickly, lest she start again on how rich he was. "It's a big house, you know."

She rolled her eyes and started out the door.

"It's not my fault it's a big house," Alan protested to her retreating back.

His father was in the kitchen, reading the paper. When Alan came in, followed by Juliet, he got to his feet. He shook Juliet's hand and directed her towards the bathroom. When she had gone, he sat back at the kitchen table and looked at his son with a raised eyebrow.

"When Trish said you were bringing someone home for

dinner, I didn't know she meant the *Guess Who's Coming* variety," he said sardonically, and went back to reading.

"What's that mean?" Alan asked.

"Nothing," his father said from behind the sports page. "Go wash your hands."

After dinner they worked a little more on the dossier, adding the details about the Marc Portland envelope and the ERICA SPI package and the XY scratched onto the bench. Then they were done. When they printed it out, it was over eight pages long. Juliet read it, sitting on the edge of Alan's unmade bed. At the end she looked up and smiled.

"You can find meaning in anything, can't you?" she asked.

"Sure," said Alan breezily. "Today in the bathroom off the foyer there were two of Trish's hairs on the sink—one of them looked like a C and one looked like a P. If I wasn't sure my father would never buy a home security system if it wasn't the best one, I would have thought CRAP was telling me they'd broken into my house."

Juliet laughed. "But what about English class?" she asked. "You know, with the poems?"

"All hairs in the sink," said Alan airily.

Juliet dug into her backpack for a notebook, then began scribbling. She ripped off a page and handed it over to him.

"What's this?" he asked her.

"A poem I read somewhere."

Alan read:

When the greasy banknotes climb upon the garden
  wall
And the banks are covered with slime and mold
And the apples are rotten in the barrels
The village idiot sings an opera
We sit and spin our tales
Waiting for the last boat home.

"So," challenged Juliet, "what do you say? What does it mean?"

"Wait a second," said Alan, reading the poem over. "Well, first of all, we have this theme of money as corrupting—*greasy* and *slime* and *mold*, and climbing on the garden wall like something unwholesome, slugs, snails, you know . . . and nature is sort of controlled by money, so we have a garden, but it's behind a wall, and covered with this snail money. And the word *apple*—well, it's so close to the word *garden* that I guess you have to read it like the apple in the garden of Eden—like we've taken the apple from the tree of knowledge and are just hoarding it, not using it, and it's rotting away. And the *banks* are probably the money banks, but it's a little ambivalent—I mean, ambiguous. It could be the riverbanks or the money banks, and the fact that it's not clear shows how money corrupts the way we see nature. Now, as to the rest, it sounds like we're just waiting for death, the last boat home, and doing nothing with our time, just sitting and spinning tales, like we're waiting, not doing. I'm not sure about the village-idiot part. I suppose it could be that we're all going on and on about how life is so tragic and all that, like some stupid opera. That's probably it. So it says that we waste our time on earth going after money, which is stupid; we ignore our opportunities for knowledge, which is stupid; we think our stupid problems are important, which is stupid, and we don't do anything about it but wait around to die: also stupid. There, done. What do you think?"

"Wow," she said. "You totally can find meaning in anything, can't you?" He glowed under her praise. It *was* amazing, this secret power of his.

And then she went and ruined it. "That was amazing— I just totally made that poem up, right now."

Alan suddenly found he was blushing. He felt tricked, exposed, like she'd pulled the curtain away just when he was in the middle of his most impressive trick. Juliet knew that now his brilliant ability to see meaning in words and between words was nothing more than crap. His cheeks burned with humiliation.

"Sink hair," he managed to choke out.

"So *that's* how you do it, with CRAP and all. You can connect the dots no matter where they are. No wonder you're so good at the game."

"The game?"

"Yeah—the SRU game." She motioned to the dossier on his desk. "No wonder Roberta chose you as the leader!"

"So you're sure it's just a game?" he asked her, trying to keep it nonchalant. "You don't think there's *anything* in it, not even after you heard the Boss today?"

"Of course not," she said. "But you *almost* convinced me. You really are good."

After she left, he looked back over the poem. It was impossible for him not to see in it the condemnation of capitalism and the sense of loss and waste he'd seen at first, and the perfection of his analysis made him feel sick to his stomach. He thought back to all the poems he had interpreted in Mrs. Perry's English class, and he was no more certain of his analysis of Countee Cullen or the John Donne bell-tolling poem than he was of the meaning in Juliet's banknote crap. He turned to the dossier they had labored over. It was a piece of crap, too, not even as well written as he'd thought it was. No wonder Alice and Keith had made fun of the game. It was stupid, all hairs in the sink. There was no truth to it at all, and Alan Green was a big fat nudnik dork for ever having considered that there was.

T HE BANKNOTE POEM BOTHERED HIM right through Sunday night and into Monday. Through all his classes he kept thinking about his interpretation, and it made everything his teachers told him seem suspect. How could you ever know that you were reading the facts right? After English he hung back, waiting for Mrs. Perry to finish shuffling her papers and notice that he was standing there.

"Yes, Alan?" she asked. "Don't you have somewhere to go?"

"Yeah, but Mrs. Perry . . . ?"

"Yes, but Mr. Green . . . ?"

"I wanted to ask you something." She listened very intelligently as he told her about the poem, and then she smiled.

When he saw she wasn't laughing at him, he went on. "Doesn't that kind of, I don't know, just say we see the meaning we want to—like that there's no real meaning out there? I thought words were supposed to mean something, not change each time someone new reads them. I thought words were supposed to last forever!"

"Hardly," said Mrs. Perry, picking up Juliet's creation again. "But if it's any consolation, I can't really say this poem really has the *beauty* of carefully crafted verse—no offense to Juliet. And beauty matters. For me, it's what makes life worth living. Juliet's poem may have given you meaning, but a great poem can give you meaning and beauty at the same time, even when it's telling you that nothing lasts." And she recited:

I met a traveller from an antique land
Who said: Two vast and trunkless legs of stone
Stand in the desert. Near them, on the sand,
Half sunk, a shattered visage lies, whose frown,
And wrinkled lip, and sneer of cold command,
Tell that its sculptor well those passions read
Which yet survive, stamped on these lifeless things,
The hand that mocked them and the heart that fed.
And on the pedestal, these words appear—
"My name is Ozymandias, king of kings:
Look on my works, ye Mighty, and despair!"
Nothing beside remains. Round the decay
Of that colossal wreck, boundless and bare
The lone and level sands stretch far away.

"I like that," Alan said. "'Nothing beside remains.' I like that one a lot."

"It's a great poem," Mrs. Perry agreed. "'Ozymandias,'

by Percy Bysshe Shelley. I'll write it out for you. Leave it in your bathroom, and you can memorize it when you're using the john."

Most teachers didn't say things like that, but Mrs. Perry did, and Alan liked her for it. He took the yellow piece of paper home and taped it over the toilet, and it made him feel a little better.

And maybe Perry was right. Maybe Alan had been connecting dots and thinking he'd seen real patterns instead of the mere meaningless workings of his mind; maybe he'd been seeing meaning and menace where no meaning or menace existed. But as Perry said, there was still beauty, and beauty was important, and Juliet was both important and beautiful. So that made up his mind.

The more and more he thought about it, the more he had become convinced that what he wanted was for her to promise to be his girlfriend. Every night that week he marshaled the troops of his courage as he lay in bed; each morning in school he watched the troops desert one by one. He planned his attack for Wednesday, during their shared Early Lunch of Losers.

He was ready. They met at the door of the cafeteria, the troops waiting for the right moment for their attack. Juliet followed him down the lunch line, so close that her shoulder almost brushed his ear. Then she followed him to a table, their table, sitting right next to him though all the other chairs were available. How could the troops discount such evidence? He hurried them into formation for their mission.

"Listen," he said. "I want to tell you . . ."

"Yes?"

And there they went, the treacherous deserters! Every last shred of his nerve had gone AWOL. "I'm glad I have the Early Lunch of Losers with you," he concluded lamely.

He cursed himself all the way up the stairs back to earth science, where he had to endure the silent treatment from frigid Alice. He glared at her. Didn't she see how he could have used a little encouragement? Instead she froze him, only speaking to ask him to pass her the powder for the stupid experiment they were doing. It was a ridiculous waste of time. He could have been using it to lure back the troops. But in the end, he sent them in unprepared.

"Listen," he blurted out when he and Juliet were alone in the culvert. "Listen, we need to talk. I have to ask you—I mean, I want to ask you, I want to say—look, what I'm saying is, what I want to know is—will you go out with me?"

It was just like in the cartoons, his legs wheelbarrowing up there in space as he desperately tried to make it back to the cliff he'd run over. He snuck a look at her face and saw only the shark-infested waters below. She would not look at him. "I *am* out with you," she said, looking the other way. The little cartoon Alan turned green, flailed one more time, and fell.

"You know what I mean," he protested from somewhere deep under the water.

"Alan . . . ," she said sorrowfully, "I don't want you to ask me that."

This was bad, very very bad, the very reason people didn't do stupid things like ask "Will you go out with me?" He felt thoroughly sick now.

"Why not?" he demanded, falling back on anger.

"Because I don't want to have to hurt your feelings. Alan, sit down, don't go—"

He hadn't realized he was pulling away, but yet he was, staggering with the blow.

"Why not?" Oh, it was bad, bad, bad, bad, bad, bad, bad, so thoroughly bad it was unbearable.

"Because we should talk about this."

"No, I mean, why won't you go out with me? I thought you liked me!"

"I *do* like you, Alan, I like you a lot, you know I do, I just—"

"What?" He noticed she had gone back to calling him by his real name.

"I just don't know if I like you *that way*—I don't even know if I *want* to like you *that way*."

"Well, why the hell not?"

"You can't control the way you feel, you know, Alan." How true! How true! He would do anything to feel differently from the way he did now, devoured by sharks.

"I just don't think it's a good idea," she went on mournfully. "And even if I *did* like you *that way*, I wouldn't want to. I care too much about you, Alan. I don't want to go out and then break up and lose you as a friend."

"What's so great about being friends?" he sputtered.

"This is what I mean," she sighed. "*This* is why—*this*, Alan."

"What?"

"This is what would happen. We'd go out, and then have some stupid fight, and then, boom, never be friends again. Just like you and Alice."

"Alice and I never went out."

"You think you'd be a better boyfriend than a friend?"

That hurt him; he winced.

"I don't want to talk about Alice," he blustered. "I just want to understand why you don't like me enough to go out with me."

"You're *totally* missing the point, Alan—I'm telling you I like you *too much* to go out with you."

This was ridiculous; if his heart hadn't been so achingly raw and hollow, he would have laughed.

"Let me get this straight," he started, but she cut him off.

"*Please* drop it, Alan," she said. "You *won't* get it straight. You'll twist it and get all mad at me and not want to be friends and then it will all be over. I won't let you, Alan Green, I won't let you ruin our friendship, because I need it!"

There was a lump in his throat now, a lump so hard and large he could barely breathe. And down below, down where his heart used to be, there was a big gaping wound where something deeply rooted had just been ripped out.

"Is there someone else?" he choked.

She didn't answer.

"I said, is there someone else?"

"I heard you," she said. "Oh, Alan, can we please not have this conversation?"

"Just tell me," he said, his eyes burning.

"You don't want to know," she answered.

He staggered; his eyes swam.

"Who is it?" he asked, thickly.

"His name is Connor Bumpass."

"Connor *Bump*ass? You mean the basketball player? What is he, a junior? Where did you even *meet* him?"

"My mother works with his father. He—he's been over a couple of times."

"Connor Bumpass!" Alan said again, as if that were some sort of condemnation. *"Why?"*

She would not look at him. Her sneakered foot pointed, flexed, was still. "He asked me out," she answered. "And I thought . . . I thought it might be a good idea."

"I just don't know what you can possibly see in that jerk," he said.

Bad move: now she was circling the wagons, defending her choices. "He's very mature," she said. "He doesn't, you know, play *games*. And he's very driven—"

"Chauffeured, you mean," Alan answered bitterly. "A *jock!* How could you, *you*, want to go out with a sweaty stupid jock who—"

She flushed. "That's prejudiced," she said. "Just preju-diced! Everyone assumes that athletes are stupid, and it's not true. Connor works *hard*, Alan. That's one of the reasons I like him. Because it's worth it to work hard, to care enough to work hard. You don't understand, because your life's so easy. . . ."

What life was she talking about? It was plainly ridiculous to say his life was easy—it was *ludicrous, risible*. She could have his easy life, if she wanted it—he was done with it now.

". . . it's like everything's always handed to you on a silver platter, and even when it's not, you don't care enough to work for it. You breeze through school—"

Here, at least, he was on high ground. "No, I don't," he told her. "It's just English where I do well—I get a lot of B's in my other classes."

"That's what I mean. You get A's when you don't have to work for them and otherwise you accept B's because you don't care enough to work hard. That's just what I mean. You don't value anything because you don't have to work for anything. You get a hole in your coat, and it's like, 'Who cares? I'll get another one.'"

"I do too value things!" Alan burst out. "And I *don't* get everything I want!"

Tears burned in his nose; the shame of it brought bile to his throat. How could he have been so stupid, so wrong? It was impossible to reconcile her words with the day of the toe shoes, or the *I don't mind when* you *do it* day, the day the cherubim came out with their long brass trumpets and sang all around him. Where were the cherubim now? They were putting their fingers in their ears and laughing;

he could have sworn he saw one mooning him. It was all gone, all his hope and happiness. *Nothing beside remains. Round the decay/Of that colossal wreck . . . /The lone and level sands stretch far away.*

"You acted like you liked me," he said finally.

"But I *do* like you, Alan. I like you so much . . . that's what I've been saying."

"Liked me *that way*, I mean," he said bleakly. "What about . . ." But once examined in the light of day, the little pieces of evidence he had kept so carefully did not point so irrefutably to the truth as he'd thought they had. Now those little scraps of evidence seemed small and insubstantial—hairs in the sink that meant nothing. It was meaningless, life, but worse than meaningless. It made you think there was meaning, a purpose, a plan, and then it betrayed you.

All the way home his cheeks burned and stung, as if she had slapped him, and his humiliation seemed so conspicuous that he felt as if he were wearing a giant red *A* on his shirt, not for adultery, like in *The Scarlet Letter*, but for a crude seven-letter insult he called himself all the way home.

The November wind was bitter. It whipped bits of leaf and grit through the air and into his eyes. How had he let this happen? The one time he had let down his guard of cool to say the stupid words *will you go out with me?* (he grimaced with the force of his humiliation), he was shot down, destroyed, strafed, dragged behind the horses, pilloried, tortured—ah! There were no words to describe his unhappiness; he had to fall back on the wordless laments of his Eastern European forebears: *ach, ach, ach, ay, ay, ay, oy, oy, oy, oy, oy.*

He let himself in the kitchen door, prepared to slip quietly up the servants' stairs and into his room, but there, unexpected, unwanted, there was Cheryl sitting at the kitchen table drinking tea. On the fourth finger of her left hand was an enormous diamond, a diamond ring, an engagement ring. He had seen it before, of course. He knew it like the back of his mother's hand, where it had sat for the first eleven years of his life.

"Hello," said Cheryl brightly. But she was scared; he could smell the fear on her. Well, let her be scared, the bitch, sitting there in Trish's seat, and wearing his mother's ring. How dare she steal from the dead like that, goddamn grave robber!

"That's my mother's ring," he informed her.

Cheryl glanced guiltily down at her left hand and gave a nervous little giggle, *hmm huh hum.* The giggle was like the straw that broke the camel's back. Alan was disgusted.

"You shouldn't be wearing my mother's ring," he stated.

"I didn't think—" she started. No, of course not. How could she think? She was a dimwit featherheaded bimbo, unequipped with the requisite apparatus for thought. How could his father stand her? She wasn't even pretty, and yet his mother hadn't been dead *two months* before his father had traded in her memory for this, this stupid . . . He ran up to his bathroom and spat out the word, the worst word he knew. He felt sick to his stomach. He huddled there in the corner, leaning his head against the cold porcelain of the toilet tank. And then he cried. He cried so hard and so long he found himself puking up everything he had eaten since that Early Lunch of Losers only six hours before, back when everything had seemed okay.

ALAN WAS LYING FACEDOWN on the sheepskin bath mat when he woke up in the morning. He got up, painfully, and staggered to the sink. "I've got a goddamn misery hangover," he said to his bloodshot reflection. He rubbed his aching temples and swaggered a bit before the mirror. "My mouth tastes like a goddamn raccoon crawled in it and died," he drawled. The face in the mirror grimaced, and he felt the tug of it on his own cheeks—as if his face were merely the reflection of the image in the mirror. "I am descending into madness," he announced to the mirror, but the face there only grinned back at him like a death mask.

Fastidiously, he cleaned himself. He brushed his teeth and used mouthwash twice, and when he thought of the tears and the vomit of the night before, he brushed his teeth again. Then he stepped into the shower. With the help of soap and steam, he stripped away the misery and humiliation of the night before and dressed himself again in his bulletproof vest of cool *sang-froid*.

When he came out at last into his bedroom, some lovesick moron was crooning about his broken heart on the clock radio. "Don't tell *me* about it, bud," Alan called across the room. "That bell tolls for *me*." He checked in then with his battered heart; the sappy lovelorn lyrics stung but did not hurt too badly. "Put ice on it," he advised the singer. "A bit of *sang-froid*, that's what your heart needs." That was all his own heart needed—that, and to be able to get out of the house without being seen.

He made it to school still in his invisible icy shell. He moved steadily, silently, *unobtrusively*, through the halls, moving like a submarine through the waves of other people, his radar on high alert, staying clear of the paths he and Juliet had worn together.

What he needed for his planned return to normalcy was to excise the previous month. He needed his old gang back, with Jethro and Keith acknowledging him as master, unsentimental Alice to keep him in line, and even a little hero worship from Agnes: all to the good. And there they were, grouped around Keith's locker, conveniently together.

"Hello, children!" he greeted them heartily. They turned to face him like one unbroken wall of—of what? He had never seen that expression on their faces before.

"What's happenin'?" he tried.

"As if you care," said Alice, turning her back on him.

"What's that supposed to mean? Of course I care!"

"That's a laugh. What happened? Did Juliet finally realize what a jerk you are?"

Alan felt his face burning. "Come on, Al," he began again, feigning an ease he no longer felt. "Don't be like that."

"Like what?" she inquired icily. "Like someone who notices when her best friend starts acting like a bastard? Or did you think I didn't notice you haven't spoken to me in weeks?"

"It hasn't been *weeks*," muttered Alan.

"Just forget it," said Alice. "We're not like some dolls you can put into a closet and pull out again when you want to play with us. We're tired of your selfishness."

His *sang-froid* was boiling with indignation now. He hated her. His two fists itched to hit her.

"I'll talk to you later," he said to Jethro and Keith, forgetting for a moment that they were on her side. "I can't talk to this . . . harpy." And he stormed down the halls.

The black cloud that hung over him made it impossible to see; he nearly ran into Juliet.

"I was looking for you," she said.

"Why? To make me feel worse?"

"Alan," she said, laying her hand on his arm. Well, his heart was frozen, or killed dead; the electricity that used to run from her fingertips deep into his core was gone, replaced only with nausea. "*Please*, Alan," she said. "I can't help how I feel."

"I couldn't help how I felt, either," he declared.

"We're still friends, right?" she pleaded.

He didn't answer.

She was actually crying now, and he was glad. It was an ugly feeling.

"What can I do?" she asked him, in anguish.

"You can't do anything," he said. He jerked his locker open and its overstuffed contents spilled out all over the ground, like a messy fountain of his rage. A few students clapped, desultorily, as they did when someone spilled a tray in the cafeteria, and a few stepped right on his things as they passed. "Just leave me alone!" he told Juliet, kneeling on the floor as he tried to order his papers again among the unfeeling feet that surrounded him. A pair of muddy boots stepped on his English essay; a pair of sneakers stomped on his little finger, but worst of all was the pair of brown shoes that stood next to the Boss's crumpled package of American Spirit cigarettes. It was a large pair of cheap brown shoes with no style to them at all: Guidance Counselor Kellerman's shoes. The unbearable day had just become unbearably worse.

"Look, give me an X-ray," Alan begged, after Kellerman had been at him for twenty minutes about the seriousness of underage smoking. "Then you'll see my lungs are as pink and clean as a goddamn baby's bottom."

"Language," said Kellerman mildly. He leaned back in his swivel chair and looked at Alan with satisfaction: a bloated spider eyeing the entangled fly.

Alan slumped in exasperation against the hard chair.

"I *told* you," he begged. "It's just part of a game."

"Cigarettes are hardly a game," Kellerman observed sententiously.

"I wasn't *smoking* them—I was *spy*ing on the person who was smoking them. Aw, forget it—you're not going to understand."

"Try me," said Kellerman. "I am capable of understanding some things—I *do* have a Ph.D. in psychology, you know."

Alan let that one slide.

"Look, we were pretending to be spies, all right?" he explained, trying by the extreme disinterest in his voice to show that he knew that playing spies was stupid and baby-ish and that he would have mocked the hell out of anyone else who did it. "We were spying on this dude who smoked these. These were *evidence*."

Kellerman resettled his hammy thighs on his chair. He was a large man, and his thighs spread out like deflated tires wrapped in cheap brown cloth as the buttons on his yellow shirt strained against his belly. He interlaced his sausage fingers and nodded wisely. "Very creative," he said. "Well, for the moment, let us accept as a postulate that these are not yours. Let us move on to another topic—your mood today, Alan. You seem upset. I'm curious to know why you seem so angry."

"I seem angry because I *am* angry," Alan explained. "Can I go now?"

"Alan, Alan," Kellerman began, shaking his head slowly. "I believe you know our school has a zero-tolerance policy towards drugs and cigarettes?"

"You just said that you believed I wasn't smoking them!"

Kellerman raised a flabby hand. "Listen to my proposal. Why don't we say I will conveniently *forget* the cigarettes and in exchange you will come here once a week and explore with me *why* you're so angry."

Oh, man! This was a million times worse than expected.

"That's not fair," Alan said. "You can't pull me in here for one thing and then get me for something else . . . that's double jeopardy!"

"No it's not," answered Kellerman smugly. "Double jeopardy is when you are tried twice for the same crime; this is more like being pulled over for a broken taillight and being arrested for drunk driving."

"I wasn't drinking, either!" Alan said, louder than he'd meant to.

"No, no, you misunderstand me. Let us say it's as if you went into the doctor's with a broken arm and he discovered you have a heart condition. It's perfectly reasonable for him to treat that, even though you came in for something else."

Alan scowled.

"So, as I was saying, I can't help but observe that you seem very agitated. Would you care to discuss what has made you so particularly angry this morning?"

"I don't have time for this," said Alan, standing.

"Well, then," Kellerman went on, unperturbed. "Let's figure this out when you *do* have time. When are your study periods? Do you happen to have one during third or sixth on Thursdays?"

"Sixth," Alan groaned. Wildly, he looked around for something to help him. There was a picture on the wall of the high school basketball team from the year Josiah Quincy had won the state championship, with Connor "I work so hard" Bumpass posing with a ball under his arm. *I'm persecuted, that's what I am,* Alan moaned. With a sigh, he turned back to the task at hand of answering every question with a monosyllabic monotone.

He felt shaken when the ringing of the bell released him from Kellerman's office. Not even the fact that he had managed to miss forty minutes' worth of Dr. Mann's pearls of wisdom soothed his jangled nerves: his equilibrium was all out of whack. All of it—Kellerman, Alice, Juliet, Cheryl, his dead mother—it all swirled around him, making him dizzy. With humiliation and despair, he remembered how he had screamed at Cheryl the night before, and how he had locked himself into his bathroom to wail and vomit like a goddamn baby, and he felt weak in the knees. He did not want to go back home and have to listen to his father's reprimands or to Trish's sympathies; what he really wanted was to climb under a rock.

He remembered just after his mother had died, after he had punched the window and spent three hours in the emergency room having them pull the glass fragments out of his hand. Keith's mother had come as soon as Keith had called her, and without asking upsetting questions had loaded them into her car and taken him to the emergency room. When the doctors were done sewing Alan up, she had brought him home to her house. That was back when they had still lived in the old house, back before Trish was there; Mrs. Reese probably thought he'd rot there before his father remembered to come home. She had taken Alan home and tucked him into Keith's bed and turned out the lights, and she had sat there and stroked his hair until he'd fallen asleep. He stayed there two days, and it had been very pleasant, all in all, what with her bringing him treats and comic books and shooing Keith out of the room every time she thought Alan needed some sleep. Now he longed for that cool room again, with its shades all drawn: what he needed was a period of convalescence.

He ran into Keith on the way to English. He punched him jovially on the arm and began to talk very quickly. His own voice irritated his ears, too loud and too fast, and he tried to calm it. "So whatcha doing this afternoon?" he concluded, just as they were entering Mrs. Perry's class-room.

"I'm busy."

"Well, maybe I'll come and be busy with you."

"No," Keith said, loud enough that several other kids turned around and stared. "No, Alan, I'm going to be busy by myself." Some giggles at that, but Keith ignored them. "I'm tired of dealing with all your crap."

"My *crap?*" Alan echoed. He stood there like a moron, waiting for the words *your crap* to stop rebounding through his empty head like balls in a pinball machine, waiting for them to go by his fumbling flippers and disappear down some hole to nowhere. Then he sat. Something touched his arm. He knew that touch; it was Juliet. He shrugged her off and sat in the corner, throwing his bag on the seat beside him so he could be alone. *I am descending into madness*, he said to himself again, and there was some comfort in that.

There was nothing to do after school. Round the decay of the colossal wreck of his life, he felt the afternoon stretching far away. *I really am going mad*, he said to himself. *I am going mad in my solitude.* The wild winds whistled in his ears, and their lonely lament was the perfect accompaniment for his mood. He plowed forward through the wind, not knowing where he was going. He staggered like a soldier through a no-man's-land, the sound of the guns pounding in the distance.

His feet had taken him to the culvert. Dead leaves blew from one side of it to the other. Alan chastised himself bitterly as he thought of the ghosts who had once shared it with him: Alice and the rest acknowledging him as their leader, Juliet on the *I don't mind when* you *make them fall asleep* day. All that was gone now. They weren't even ghosts there anymore, just shadows of ghosts.

He sat down in the leaves and leaned back against the

curving wall of the culvert, feeling the rough concrete catching at his hair. What had happened to his comfortable, tolerable life? It all sucked now. Before he had had a posse that had followed him around and protected him from the self-satisfied frogs like Rory Frankel, and now even stupid Keith Reese the Obese could stand there and humiliate him in front of everyone. Once he had cool gorgeous Ballerina Juliet hanging on his arm, and now she had abandoned him, too. Once, at least, he had had quiet at home, alone with Trish—as usual he had only learned to appreciate her when it was too late.

Yes, it was just like Mrs. Perry had said in that Yeats poem: *Things fall apart, the center cannot hold.* But how had everything fallen apart so quickly? He felt as if he had found a little string sticking out of the sweater of his life, and he had barely tugged at it before the whole thing had unraveled. It unraveled completely until he stood there, naked, everyone laughing at him, and still the sweater kept unraveling until his skin opened up and all his entrails poured out onto the ground. How stupid he looked, standing there, staring at his entrails, as Alice and Keith and Juliet and Kellerman stood around and clapped.

Are those my guts?

Those are your guts, sucker!

Alan closed his eyes. It wasn't so much fun, all this going crazy. Wearily, he picked himself up and started home. He trudged up the back stairs and sat on the edge of his bed without even turning on the light to ward off the November dusk. It was just *insupportable, untenable,* all of it, Juliet, Alice, Kellerman, Cheryl, Cincinnati— with a cry of frustration, he let himself fall backwards onto the pillow. He closed his eyes against the dark, and there, like Countee Cullen, hid the heart that bleeds.

NOW HE KNEW HOW KAUFMAN FELT. For the first time since he could remember, Alan Green was not *unobtrusive*. Everything was different now that his friendless state made him conspicuously alone.

It was worst at lunchtime. The bell would ring, and all the stupid happy people would hurry out. They streamed out of their classrooms like tributaries looking for rivers that lead to the sea; rivers that joined up with friends and boyfriends and girlfriends, all making their way down to the cafeteria, while Alan alone among dorks tasted the unpleasant tang of loneliness. John Donne was wrong about one thing: at least one man was an island, and that man was Alan Green, all alone in an inhospitable sea.

He was nearly the last in line, he walked so slowly, and he dragged his tray along the cafeteria counter, looking without interest at the slop they slapped on his plate. The worst moment was when he turned the corner from the kitchen into the lunchroom and was met by the wall of sound of the self-admiring bog. There was nowhere to sit among the croaking frogs that did not seem horribly conspicuous: not the area near the door, which looked like he was trying to run away, not the area near the wall where the losers sat, and certainly not near Juliet in the middle. He found a seat and began shoveling in his lunch. He ate so quickly he had a pain in his chest, as if the grilled cheese had lodged there sideways.

The pain didn't go away by the period after lunch, either, and he began to worry. *I'm having a heart attack*, he thought. There it was: that squeezing pain again. He broke into a sweat, looking for a sympathetic face. Alice sat with her back to him, stony and cold, like an ice sculpture. She wouldn't care if he just keeled over and died right there. He had no idea what the symptoms of a heart attack were, although he'd heard they included "a sense of imminent doom." Well, he had that all right. What should he do? A heart attack wasn't something you could just put an ice pack on; you couldn't walk it off; if you waited it out, you'd be dead. His sweat felt cold on his forehead. What was he going to do? Raise his hand and ask to be excused to go to the hospital? Everyone would laugh. It was ridiculous. He was going to die here, at his desk, here in stupid Spanish class, just because he was too scared to be embarrassed. *Voy a morir*, he thought to himself, and then, because they were studying the future tense, *moriré*. He felt light-headed. He couldn't draw a deep breath. That was probably a sign of heart attack, too. He forced himself to breathe deeper. In. Out. In. Out.

Out. Out. Out. What if he couldn't breathe in again? What if the pain in his chest was a collapsed lung? Were his lips turning blue already? He could feel them buzzing. Oh, crap! He really was going to die. He would pass out at his desk with his tongue protruding out of his blue lips, and they would all laugh at him. He could hear them, now. He *could* hear them now. He looked up: the whole class was staring at him.

"*Por favor, Señor Verde, no está tiempo para la siesta. ¿Por qué no quiere María ir a la escuela con su hermana?*"

He stared at Señora Flatbush blankly. "I have to go to the nurse," he blurted out.

"*¡En español, por favor!*"

"*Tengo que ir a la* nurse."

Señora Flatbush considered; she looked at the clock and at Alan, sweating in his seat, and said. "*Bien. Váyate. Hasta mañana.*" She turned back to the class and contin-ued asking stupid questions up and down the aisles, treat-ing them all like retarded kindergartners. Alan was out of there in a flash.

The nurse said she thought he was having a panic attack. She said he should drink a nice big glass of water and lie down, but Alan shook his head—it hurt too much just to be in his mind. But the nurse assured him that the brain was a mighty organ capable of convincing itself and the body of anything, and told him to lie down for a while. To his surprise Alan discovered it was very pleasant to be lying there on the vinyl-covered cot, breathing in the soothing smell of antiseptic in the comforting quiet. The nurse brought him a cup of apple juice, and together with the feel of the vinyl next to his cheek, the smell of it reminded him agreeably of nursery school. *Maybe I should just go back to being four again*, he thought. *Maybe I should just start over.*

He did not feel better, not the next morning, nor all that weekend. The problem was that home was no better than school, now that his haven had been invaded. It was still a shock to see Cheryl sitting at the kitchen table, all dainty and perfect and irritating. Even at seven in the morning, she was showered, powdered, buffed, and polished. Trish stood behind her in her old ratty bathrobe, hair all tousled by sleep and stupid-looking, pouring batter into the hot waffle iron while Cheryl lifted a piece of waffle to her mouth. She leaned forward a little, to make sure no syrup dripped onto her clothing, and she pulled her lips back wide to make sure she did not mess up her lipstick before poking the fork into her mouth. Everything she did was profoundly annoying. Alan couldn't stand her perkiness, or the way she ended each sentence with her awkward *hmm huh hum* laugh that sounded like a horse choking on a whinny.

"The drapers are coming this afternoon," she would announce, or "The painters should be here this morning," or "If anyone wants to look at wallpaper samples, I've got a book in the study *hmm huh hum*."

Worst of all was what she had done to his house. Within moments of her crossing the threshold, it seemed, Alan's interesting, empty home was being stupidified with clutter and junk. The clean, empty living room was now an eye-jarring cacophony of cabbage roses: cabbage roses on the wallpaper, on the drapes, even on the new couches and chairs. It was all of a piece, decorating by catalog, as if Cheryl had pointed a painted fingernail at a picture in a magazine, and said, "I'd like a new living room, please. This one." Now when people came over and said, "Man, your house is so *big*," they would not be able to laugh at how weird it was that it was so empty; they would not be able to rattle around in it like it was some mysterious abandoned mansion. Now when they came over and said, "Man, your house is so *big*," they would mean only that he was rich. If anyone ever came over again, that was. He fled to Trish's room.

"This is *unbearable*," he announced.

"What is?"

"What Cheryl's doing. The house looks totally stupid."

"I think it's nice it's getting some attention," Trish said. "At least the rooms don't echo anymore."

"That's because she's filling them with crap," said Alan. "Why didn't *you* decorate it? Then it could look like *this* and not like some tacky ad for room fresheners." And he waved his hand to encompass all her knickknacks and bric-a-brac.

"As I recall, you said my room looked like a flea market

when you first saw it. I believe you were quite rude about it."

"But I didn't mean it. And anyway, the room is growing on me." He looked down at the Turkish kilim on the floor, all rough and musty. She was right: he didn't really want her to decorate the whole house like a Turkish flea market, either. He just wanted it to be the way it was, before. He wanted *everything* to be the way it was before, with his friends and Trish and everything normal. Several times his hand hovered over the phone as if instinctively reaching out to call Alice, the way he always had when he was in trouble. He remembered the day he called her and started blubbering because he couldn't say the terrible words about his mother, and how she had come right over and sat with him on the stoop of his old house and held his hand. He remembered her as Agent 55378008, madly writing down license plates of SUVs and interpreting them with inspired lunacy. Oh, Alice! All he wanted was to get back to the way everything was before. Was that too much to ask?

But everything was different, as if the universe wanted Alan to die the death of a thousand cuts. Dinnertime, for example, had gone from unpleasant to dreadful. Even Cheryl had a hard time keeping conversation afloat. His father, beetled brows bent low over his plate, said nothing as he shoveled food into his mouth like a steam shovel. Trish tried to beat off the silence that emanated from the Green males, but her attempts at lighthearted banter always failed, and the conversation, weighed down by silence, grew harder and harder to volley back and forth. They subsided into silence again: eighteen past the hour.

Then Trish tried again with a topic she knew would get them all going.

"I talked to Myra Kaufman today. She said Morris was beat up again after school."

It worked: everyone looked up, even Alan.

"That's terrible!" said Cheryl, as if she knew him. "What happened?"

"What always happens," Alan told her. "Rory Frankel and his gang jumped him on the way home. I guess the karate lessons aren't paying off."

"Alan," said Trish, in a voice that made him suddenly feel small and ashamed. "That was a cruel thing to say."

"Sorry," he mumbled.

"What a disappointment to George," said Alan's father. He turned to Cheryl and explained: "I know that kid's father—a good guy—we play racquetball sometimes. What an embarrassment, to have his son be the punching bag of the junior high."

"I think he'd be more worried than embarrassed, Mitch," said Cheryl gently.

Alan stared; he hadn't expected her to say something like that. And the worse part was, he'd felt just like his father. The fact of the matter was that it *was* embarrassing, the way Kaufman kept on getting beaten up. There were times you just wanted to smack him and tell him to pull himself together. Alan asked to be excused.

Trish followed him up into his room after dinner. "What's wrong, Alan?" she asked him. "You seem, I don't know, *down*, somehow."

"I don't know."

"Do you want to talk?"

"Not particularly."

"Let me rephrase that," she said. "What do you want to talk about?"

"I just feel depressed." He threw himself backwards on the bed. "Trish," he said to the ceiling, "tell me you're not really going."

Tentatively, Trish reached out and ruffled his hair.

"This isn't my home, Alan," she said. "It never was, and I never expected it would be. I only sublet my apartment back in Cincinnati, and I can go back in January."

"How can you do this to me?" he demanded.

Trish leaned down and kissed the top of his head.

"Because we all have to grow up sometime, Alan," she said.

Grow up: he wished he could. He would have given anything to wake up one morning and discover that junior high school was behind him. Things only got worse. On Monday morning, for example, Alice was not at their table when Alan arrived at earth science. Instead, she was sitting next to some new kid across the room, and she didn't come back to their table when class began.

"Hey!" Alan cried indignantly when he found himself alone.

"Ellie didn't have a partner," Alice explained coldly, from where she sat.

"But now *I* don't!"

"Well, that should suit you just fine, shouldn't it?"

Alan turned to Keith for support, but Keith was studiously reading a comic book under his table and wouldn't look up at all.

"Mr. Andrews!" Alan complained. "How am I supposed to do the lab alone?"

Mr. Andrews shrugged. "Pretend you have a partner who doesn't do any work," he suggested tiredly. "Lots of people in this class do the labs alone. Right, folks?" Mr. Andrews looked as if he had slept in his clothes. There was a bit of dried egg on his tie—it was all very sordid and depressing.

"I think I have to go to the nurse," Alan mumbled. He picked up his things and headed out the door.

He lay on the nurse's couch, listening to the thuds and scraping sounds of the classroom above. Then he went back to English, and to math. When the bell rang for lunch, he started down the lonely river in despair. Suddenly he scrambled back up onto the bank. In a moment, he was back at the nurse's, his cheek pressed comfortably against the purple vinyl of the bed.

"I can't reach your aunt."

"Huh?" He had been thinking about something else, something comforting and familiar and very far away, like being read to on his mother's lap.

"I can't reach your aunt. Do you think you feel well enough to go back to class?"

Alan considered. "Maybe," he said. "Can I come back later, if I need to?"

Miscalculation: the nurse looked confused. "Are you planning on feeling sick?" she asked.

"I might," he told her.

"But your friends will miss you!"

So she wasn't the sharpest knife in the drawer. In the knife drawer of life, this nurse was a chopstick.

"That's a laugh," he told her. "A real sidesplitter. Have you thought about going out for stand-up? Because you've got it—you really do." She stared at him blankly. He tried to explain. "Look, I just like knowing I can come here."

"We're not really set up for that," she objected. "We're really for kids who are sick. I don't think you're really ill."

Ah, that's where you're wrong, sister, he told her in his head. *I am desperately sick, sick at heart. Terminally, probably.*

"And you're not going to get better hiding here," she told him, and then she cast him out into the sea of scorn that was the rest of Josiah Quincy Junior High.

Of course, there was one person at school who still wanted to talk to Alan. He had been hoping Kellerman wouldn't remember, but there he was, waddling through the tables in the cafeteria during sixth-period study hall that Thursday, sniffing Alan out. He stood over Alan, a false smile plastered onto his doughy face, and waited. Alan said nothing. He felt like some small animal, freezing in the headlights, hoping the car wouldn't barrel down on him.

"Well, Alan," Kellerman wheezed, "it's Thursday! Did you forget our date?"

Oh, worse! worse! worse! The giggles came from all around him, sticking to him like feathers on tar as Kellerman marched him through the bog, his hammy hand burning on Alan's shoulder: he would never be *unobtrusive* again. And now he was sitting on the hard plastic seat watching Kellerman arrange his belly on his thighs and apply his Ph.D. to understanding Alan. His chest hurt.

"I hear from the nurse you've been spending a lot of time in her office," Kellerman began, pressing his fingertips together and flexing and unflexing his fingers. *What's this? A spider doing push-ups on a mirror.*

"I haven't been feeling well."

"Ah."

A long silence, intended to be significant.

"Don't read too much into it," Alan said.

"Wouldn't dream of it," Kellerman answered, with his insufferable faint and superior smile. "Now, we don't have very much time together as you . . . let us say, *forgot* our little appointment. I spoke to your father at length yesterday, Alan. He said that you are very upset about his upcoming marriage. I just want you to know that I'm here to *listen*. That's my real job here, to be a friendly pair of ears." He grinned pretentiously, and the friendly pair of ears wiggled.

"Neat trick," said Alan sullenly.

"So tell me," Kellerman went on, ignoring the sarcasm. "Do you think the idea of a stepmother bothers you because it seems like a betrayal of your mother?" He paused. "Or perhaps you wonder if your father would forget *you* so quickly if it had been *you* who had died?"

"You've got to be kidding me," groaned Alan. "Where did you get this Ph.D. of yours? Off the back of a box of Sigmund Freudios?"

He sighed heavily and looked away. His eye fell on the twelve-month school calendar that had been pinned to the wall. There was an infinite series of Thursdays there, all leading down like rungs on a one-way ladder to hell.

It was easiest to breathe outside. Alan took to wandering the streets in the afternoon, shuffling through the dried leaves. While he walked, he talked to Juliet in his head.

So you won't go out with me because you're worried we won't be friends.

That's right. It all would make sense if you weren't such an idiot, Alan.

So let me get this straight. You think if we don't go out, we'll be friends, then?

Yes.

Not much of friends now, are we?

They weren't. He barely talked to her in class or the halls anymore; it was too painful, too humiliating. Sometimes she tried—she slipped him notes in English, called him at home—but he didn't want to talk to her. The betrayal was too raw—Connor Bumpass! Connor *Bump*ass! And everyone knew. He picked her up after school on Mondays and Wednesdays now in his stupid I'm-a-big-fancy-basketball-player *car*. They walked hand in hand out towards the parking lot, a head taller than everyone else, and people Alan didn't even know stopped him in the halls and said, "I thought *you* were going out with Ballerina Juliet." Even Rory Frankel, putting in one of his rare appearances in school, commiserated with Alan about it, punching him fraternally on the arm and saying *"Sucker."*

Screw you, Ballerina Juliet! Alan screamed at her in his head.

The culvert was his only haven, now, out of sight of prying, judging eyes. Alan walked there, kicking at the leaves.

What are you doing here, Secret Agent Asswipe? Looking for clues for your stupid little game?

Shut up. I'm just walking.

He *was* just walking, but his wandering eye saw something there, something shiny, something yellow. He knelt down and picked it up. It was a business card: *Leonard Becker. Firearms Dealer: Antique and Rare.*

Alan stood there a moment, looking at it. Leonard Becker. Leonard. Lenny. The Henchman. He was a gun dealer, a *gun* dealer.

What, so that means he's an assassin? mocked a voice in

his head. *It's just a coincidence, and looking for meaning in coincidences is as foolish as believing in God.*

There might *be a God*, Alan answered himself. *We don't know for sure that there isn't. And if Lenny is a gun dealer, doesn't that have to mean something?*

It might not be him, the voice in his head objected. *It might be some other Leonard.*

There was only one way to be sure, and Alan had to know. He scooted down the embankment and hid in the culvert. He took his cell phone from his jacket pocket and dialed the number. It rang twice, and then the voice he had heard so many times picked up.

"Yeah?"

"Is this Lenny?"

"Yeah."

"Oh," said Alan, his heart pounding, "thank you." And he hung up. He was shaking, actually shaking. A moment later, his phone rang, displaying Trish's name. *Oh, crap!* he thought. There was no guarantee at all that when he'd called Leonard Becker, his own name and number had not been listed there for the Henchman to see—and if they knew his name, he would never be *unobtrusive* again. He turned off the phone to silence the ringing and dropped it into the leaves that carpeted the culvert.

Crap! he thought. *Oh, crap crap crap crap crap.*

But as his heart began to return to normal, he realized the import of what had just happened. It was true: Lenny the Henchman was a gunrunner, and suddenly CRAP seemed a lot more than crap.

Come on—don't be so goddamn lame! he berated himself. *It was lame enough when you did this with other people, but this is beyond lame. Lamissimo. Lame to the third degree.*

He was headed home, eyes on the ground to avoid having to meet anyone else's, when he suddenly saw something in the dry leaves of the gutter. He bent down and picked it up. It was a scrap of rain-stiffened letter, written in jelly marker on stationery with a cutesy dog on it, holding a patchwork C in its mouth, *barf barf barf.* Alan read it over once, laughing at that sap who wrote it. And then, because habits are hard to break, he involuntarily began to interpret it. As he did, his hands grew cold.

Dear Brett
Why is it that when your with your friend's your so mean to me? Why can't you be like you are when we're alone like that time you know when I mean. It just hurts me that you act so cruel it's not fair that you act like Laura Menelo's your girlfriend when you told me that it was me that was. You can be so cruel Brett your just so cold. I know your not cold in your heart tho I know you really. But you can look right through me with such cold eyes. Please be the way you were when we were together that night after pizza back in September you remember you have to remember you couldn't forget, not that night. But you walk right by me so cold I don't know how a person can do that, be one way and then such another how can

That was the whole message, artfully written as if it went on to another page. But of course there was no other page and no lovesick girl: this was a coldhearted communication from CRAP. It might even come from the highest levels of the organization to either the Boss or the Henchman—probably the Boss, since people often chose code names that looked like their real names, and both "Brett" and "Boss" started with B's and ended with double letters.

Alan started home, turning the letter over in his hands. It was obviously in code, but how? As usual, he searched for the key, the thing that stuck out. Well, here it was: the misspellings of the word *you're*, clearly designed to draw your eye to them. There were seven repetitions of the word *your*—it meant the number seven was significant. The prominent name Laura Menelo took some thought until he remembered how his prissy cousin Laura was always droning on and on about how her name meant "the dawn." (Of course, she also said "Alan" meant "cheerful," and that was obviously just a crock.) Menelo was a little more confusing until he realized he had to anagram the letters. Look, there it was: *me lone*. Me, alone, at the dawn. But for what? It must be another assassination—he'd been waiting for it since the day Juliet had overheard they'd tagged Fordham. But there was no mention of Governor Fordham by name. Or was there? Look at that, Laura Menelo: LM, consecutive letters of the alphabet, just like Erica Fordham's initials. And from E to L was seven letters—just like the seven repetitions of the word *your*—there it was! Code and key in the same letter, just like the Marc Portland envelope. And thinking of the Marc Portland envelope, he suddenly remembered the address, 1123 Lee Street. And wasn't today the twenty-third of November? It was—and that was just too much of a coincidence. His hands had begun to shake.

It's just a game, he reminded himself.

Of course it was a game—he knew it was a game—but still, it was a little creepy to find himself on the twenty-third of November just as the envelope predicted, having found this other clue. He sat down on the curb, counting out the words, and then, with a stick, he multiplied 11 and 23 together: 253. He sat back. Was it a coincidence, or not, that the letter had 153 words in it?

Hold on, Secret Agent 666—253 isn't the same as 153.

But they're so close! It has to mean something. And then, there it was. He picked up the letter again and looked at the stupid dopey stationary with the letter C. And what was C, after all, but the Roman numeral for one hundred? He sat back, stunned. It was today, then, that Lenny was going to carry out his attack.

Holy everything falling in place, Agent 666!

He was so pleased with his analysis that he forgot that the SRU was dead, kaput, its members scattered to the winds. His hand reached for his cell phone before he remembered he had left it buried in the leaves. He raced to the nearest pay phone.

"I've got it!" he shouted when Juliet answered.

"What do you mean, you've got it? Who is this? It's Alan, isn't it?"

"I found the proof!" he told her. "I found the proof that CRAP's totally behind the assassination. We—"

"Alan!" she practically screeched. 'That's not funny, Alan—it's not funny at all!"

"What?"

"Someone tried to *kill* her, Alan. Can't you see this is serious? It isn't a joke, not anymore. There really is someone out there trying to change the government."

He had no idea what she was talking about; he thought, for a passing moment, that perhaps it was she who was descending into madness. Finally she hung up, and, clutching the letter in his hands, looking for additional clues, Alan went home.

When he came into the foyer, he could see Trish in the living room, drowning in the enormous cabbage roses on the couch. Something in her still form made him pause. The lights were off, and the blue of the television's light cast flickering shadows on her stricken face.

"What's wrong?" he asked.

"Someone tried to shoot the governor," she answered in a dead voice.

For a moment, Alan assumed he must have misheard; it was a coincidence too impossible to be believed.

"No," he said, gripping the letter in his hand. "That's impossible."

He came and stood behind the couch. The news anchor was showing the tiny scrap of footage over and over; Alan saw (and saw again and again and again) that the attack had come as the governor had stepped from a helicopter not long after dawn in a remote airfield. Juliet was right; this was not funny. It was downright terrifying.

Trish looked over at him, her face a sickly blue in the wavering light. "There's nothing to panic about, Alan," she reassured him. "You don't need to worry. The police will catch—"

"They didn't catch them last time."

"Them?"

"The group that's trying to bring down the government."

"Oh, Alan! Is that what you've been worried about? The police think it's a single madman, not some sort of vast conspiracy. Assassins usually are, you know. Six presidents were shot in the first two hundred years or so of American history, and with one possible exception, none of the attacks seem to have been politically motivated in any way that wasn't entirely crazy. This is another sick, sick man, Alan. You don't need to worry. They'll catch this nut, and it will all be over. The government won't fall, and you'll be safe."

She was mostly wrong, as usual. She had no idea what was making him feel so sick to his stomach. What terrified him was that fact that he *knew*. He'd known about Murphy, and he'd known about this, and that meant CRAP was *not* crap, and worse, it made him responsible, because no one else would ever believe him. But he had to try.

As he talked, Trish's nervous look fell away, only to be replaced by a kind of melancholy amusement. "Come sit down, Alan," she said kindly. "Let me tell you a story."

Alan shifted his weight from foot to foot. He didn't

have time for this—he needed to think. He looked long-ingly towards the hall.

"Come on, Alan! Try not to look like a dog that needs to go out—I'll release you soon enough. I just think you might be interested in this story. Now listen. I suppose you know that some of planets can be seen with the naked eye. You know that, right?"

Planets? What was she, senile? This was a colossal waste of time!

"And you know that Neptune and Uranus were discovered relatively recently?"

"Sure."

"So, how did they find them?"

His father was always complaining that Alan had no manners, but this was proof that he did. If he allowed himself to do what he wanted, he would have been out of there in a flash.

"I have no idea," he told her.

"Well, astronomers predicted them. They looked at the way other astronomical objects acted, and they predicted that some unseen and very heavy objects must be there, affecting the system. And they trained their telescopes where they expected to see the objects, and voilà, there they were."

"That's great," said Alan, starting to sidle off the couch. "But I have to—"

"Calm down," Trish ordered. "I'm not done with my story, and when I'm done, *then* you can race away. Now, a hundred years or so ago, there was an amateur astronomer—a hobbyist, you might say. And this man, Percival Lowell, became obsessed with finding a ninth planet. He made all sorts of complicated calculations based on the movements of Neptune and Uranus, but they never panned out. And then someone pointed a telescope to where Lowell's calculations said there should be another heavenly body, and there it was, a little lump of something, a planet—or so they thought. And they called it Pluto, because all the other planets are named for Roman gods, and because Pluto could be abbreviated PL to honor the name of its discoverer, Percival Lowell."

"Okay," said Alan, starting to get up. "Very inspirational. Got it."

"You're missing my point," Trish said—and in this she was right. "The point is that it turned out that Lowell's calculations were based on faulty data. And even if they had been right, Pluto itself couldn't possibly be the planet Lowell's calculations predicted—it's just too small to affect other objects. Some people now say we shouldn't even count Pluto as a planet—that it's really nothing more than a glorified meteor."

Alan's left foot was twitching; he couldn't help it.

"I really have to go," he said.

"Then I'll make my point," said Trish. "Lowell's followers were so enamored of his analysis that they searched and searched until they found something, and when they found something, they convinced themselves that the object they found was what they were looking for. Lowell was wrong, Alan. His intentions were good, but he saw planets when no planets were there."

He got her point now, now that she'd hit him over the head with it. But she didn't know what she was talking about. He *had* predicted the assassination attempt. He stood up.

"Even if that Lowell dude was wrong," he declared, "he did find *something*."

"Not much of something," said Trish gently. "A rock, orbited by another rock nearly half its size—an asteroid, nothing more."

"But he found *something*," Alan repeated stubbornly. "Even if his analysis was wrong, it led him to *something*." And then he ran out of the room.

H E HAD TO TELL SOMEONE, but there was no one to tell. He tried Keith in the halls the next morning.

"Give me a break," Keith interrupted when Alan was half through.

"But you can't deny that I predicted both assassinations. . . ."

"I can't? Watch me: I'll do it again: I deny it. And again: I deeeeeenyyyyy it. How can I explain this gently, Alan? I deny it because, well—because if you were sane, you'd deny it, too." And he lumbered off.

Desperately, Alan searched the halls. There was Alice— she might hate him, but she would understand about what he had begun to call the Pluto Project in his head. She would understand it, even though it was impossible. She would see that the SRU really had uncovered a link between the Boss and the assassinations, just as Pluto had been discovered by mistake.

"I don't want to talk to you," she said as he approached.

"Well, I don't really want to talk to you, either, but I need to. Listen . . ." And he explained. When he was not quite done, she interrupted him.

"You're sick, you know that?" she said. "Really sick. One governor's been *murdered*, and they're trying to kill another one, and you're still playing this stupid fantasy? This is serious, Alan. Don't you care about people *at all?*"

"Yes!" Alan shouted. "I'm telling you *because* I care, can't you see that? I'm asking you to help *because* I know it's serious!"

"Oh, Jesus Christ," she said. "I hope one of these days you're going to realize the world wasn't invented for your amusement." She stalked away, leaving Alan alone with the weight of his responsibility.

It was crushing, that weight. He hadn't been lying when he said he cared. The fact that he had known that Fordham was in danger made him feel responsible for her life, the way you might feel if you'd been walking down the street and suddenly heard a cry coming from a Dumpster. If you looked in and found a baby there, you couldn't just leave it; you'd have to take it out and try and save it. And if you brought it to the police, and they refused to believe you, what would you do? Even if you didn't devote your life to it, you'd be haunted by guilt and doubt.

He tried to convince himself that he was wrong, but he always came back to the fact that he had guessed something was going to happen right before each of the governors had been attacked. And that was a fact that could not be denied, no matter what Keith said. And whenever he found something new—like the phone number on the back of the American Spirit cigarettes—it would all fall into place.

He had found the phone number in the culvert one afternoon towards the very end of November: 935-1219. It was written on a scrap ripped from a yellow package of American Spirits, but it wasn't a working number, not in three area codes.

Why would someone write down a phone number that doesn't work? he asked himself.

Maybe it isn't a phone number. Maybe it's supposed to look like a phone number, *just like the conversations were supposed to sound like normal conversations.*

What could it be, then? A combination?

A time. A date.

What date? Am I supposed to figure out something that happened between 935 and 1219? There's no thirty-fifth of September.

No, but there is a nineteenth of December—and thirty-five minutes past nine.

So the nineteenth of December was significant. And the thing of it was that once he knew the number nineteen was important, it started showing up everywhere. For example, it was in that XY scratched onto the bench. From X to E—counting backwards—was nineteen letters, which might mean that XY was really supposed to refer to the governor's initials. There was also the skid mark on the bridge above the culvert that was clearly in the shape of an S—and S was the nineteenth letter of the alphabet!

Even the cigarettes themselves carried a message. Take the Indian on the package of American Spirit cigarettes. How many feathers were in his headdress? Nine that you could see—which meant that there were probably nine on the other side, and one at the very top: nineteen, just like the nineteenth of December. And was it a coincidence that "American Spirit Ultra" had nineteen letters? Of course, they were really called "American Spirit Ultra Kings," but that just meant that after the nineteenth, all that would be left would be the kings—that is, the unelected leaders who would control the state. (And really, what motto better suited an ultra-libertarian male supremacist militia group like CRAP than "American Spirit Ultra Kings"?) And how had he missed it that when you anagrammed the letters of "American Spirit," you got CRAP: I a minister. CRAP, a minister—not a minister of the church, of course, but a minister of the government— CRAP was going to stage a coup. And if you anagrammed "December nineteenth" you got THE MEN NET BEND ERICE, which, far from nonsense, meant that the man net (the machinations of the women-hating CRAP) would bend Erica Fordham to their will. He sat back from his computer, staring at the anagrams that swirled on the screen.

And then, in the beginning of December, came a day that proved he was right about it all. The discovery began, ironically, with a bit of civil disobedience. In the days since the reopening of the Pluto Project, school had fallen away in importance in Alan's life. It wasn't that he wasn't interested in learning—he did spend long hours in the library, reading about codes and cryptography. He learned about the German Enigma machine that chunked chunky gears to spew out code thought to be unbreakable; he learned about the counter-codes used by the Americans that made use of the Navajo language—the Windtalkers. For good measure, he learned Morse code and Braille, in case the pockmarks in the sidewalks held raw data that should not be overlooked.

But school was not learning. At best, the lonely hours there were tedious; at worst, they were torture. One Friday, as he dragged his feet closer towards the place of incarceration, he felt he had not the strength to walk through the big orange doors. It was all too much: he turned around and left.

His feet brought him to the culvert. He walked through the leaves on the side of the road, kicking them up into the air as he shuffled through the gutter. He wandered around the back of the police station. It wouldn't surprise him in the least if CRAP had the police neatly in its back pocket. And if that were the case, that innocuous-looking date carved into the corner that declared the building had been built in MCMLV was in most likelihood some sort of defiant message, like Menacing CRAP Murders Ladies Violently.

Suddenly, his ears pricked. A car was coming.

It was a white car—the Boss's white Ford Probe, and at that moment Alan knew there was a reason he had decided to skive off school that very day. Keeping close to the ground, he dashed away from the police station, skittered down the icy embankment, and huddled there in the culvert.

Up above, the car came to a stop. The door creaked open as the Boss got out and protested as he slammed it shut. Alan heard him crunch across the bridge. He began to pace, sending small stones falling next to Alan's hiding place, and then he began to whistle. It was a haunting, menacing sound: slow and deliberate. Alan cocked his ears—he knew that tune, and knew its words: "Pop Goes the Weasel."

The Boss paced there, back and forth, whistling his slow, deliberate dirge: *All around the cobbler's bench / The monkey chased the weasel / The monkey thought it was all in good fun / Pop! goes the weasel.* Again and again he whistled it, each time slower, more contemplatively, more ominously. It made Alan's blood run cold. The Boss had taken this happy childhood ditty and turned it into a thing of menace. The piercing tune made another round, and the words ground themselves into Alan's head: *The monkey thought it was all in good fun / Pop! goes the weasel.*

It was a code: of course it was a code. The constant repetition proved that, if nothing else, not to mention the generally ominous nature of the lyrics. His brain raced—it raced in overdrive. It *must* be a secret message—and look at that, it was—just look at the second letters of the first two words—the L of ALL and the R of AROUND. What was L, after all, but the twelfth letter of the alphabet, and what was R (here Alan counted frantically on his fingers) but the eighteenth? And what was 12/18? It was the day before the nineteenth of December, and the nineteenth of December was the day CRAP planned to carry out its next attack on Erica Fordham!

But wait a minute, rein in those horses—was *Fordham* the subject of the song? He knew they had taunted her by calling her a dog, but why a weasel? Wouldn't you think CRAP would admire weasels? Or maybe the song wasn't about Fordham at all—since, when you thought about it, *she* was going to be fine on the eighteenth—it was the nineteenth she had to worry about. So who was the weasel? Was it Lenny? He certainly *sounded* like a weasel. And then, suddenly, Alan saw it all. If Lenny was the weasel, then perhaps the Boss was planning to have more than one victim at the end of December. Lenny was going to show up expecting his fat Christmas bonus, and *Pop!* goes the Lenny. *A penny for a spool of thread / A penny for a needle / That's the way the money goes / Pop! goes the weasel.* A shroud, a winding sheet, that's what they were talking about. Alan closed his eyes.

He was sure he was right. He had heard the hard edge to the Boss's voice as he had threatened Lenny: *But if it's not done then, Lenny, then you are. Done. You know what I mean.* And it wasn't done, because Erica Fordham had survived the attack on November twenty-third.

Alan's head fell back against the culvert wall. It was clear that the Boss did not look kindly on failure. He was going to let Lenny bait the trap for the nineteenth, and then he was going to do away with him—Alan was sure of it. Even if the song wasn't a code, it was some sort of Freudian window into the twisted workings of the Boss's mind. No one who had heard the Boss's "But if it's *not* done then, Lenny, then you are. Done" could hear the menace in his whistling and doubt that Lenny was in danger.

Then he heard it, the sound of Lenny's game leg dragging through the gravel. Alan almost threw up.

"I'm almost set," said Lenny, before the Boss could speak.

"I've heard that before," the Boss said drily. *Run, Lenny!* Alan pleaded. *Run while you still can.*

But Lenny didn't run; instead he tried to weasel out of his failure. "It wasn't my fault," he whined peevishly. "I was interrupted. It was the wrong place."

"And you know you have the right place now?"

"Yeah. Just like I told you."

"And we meet the night before, just like you promised?"

"The night before."

"Bring it with you," the Boss said laconically. The whistle faded away as he walked towards his car: *A penny for a spool of thread / A penny for a needle.*

Alan sat in the culvert, ramrod straight, barely breathing. The night before! The eighteenth! And he had predicted that the eighteenth was important, from the song! He had calculated that the song was about the eighteenth before he'd known that the eighteenth was important— and that was like getting evidence to support a hypothesis, and getting evidence to support a hypothesis was completely different from reading whatever he wanted into the sink hairs of his experience—it was like scientific proof. It meant he wasn't making it up—it meant it was true. But now that he knew about it, maybe he could finally do something. He could see what they were doing, watch the handoff (for "Bring it with you" obviously meant Lenny should bring proof), and maybe he, Alan Green, Secret Agent 666, might be able to thwart their plans and save Erica Fordham. He might even be able to save Lenny's life as well.

What, he said to himself. *Do I really need to worry about Lenny, too?*

Yes, answered the voice in his head, though he could not justify it. Lenny might be a thug and a weasel; he might be a gunrunner and an assassin, but he was also a sucker, and for that Alan ached for him.

For a moment, he stood there as if frozen, and then, with a *whoosh*, the breath left his body. He needed to tell someone—he needed to tell Juliet. To hell with humiliation! To hell with Connor Bumpass! He ran the whole way to her house, only stopping occasionally to press his hand to his winded side—maybe Kellerman had been right to think he was a smoker. But here was her street, and here was her house; he was hammering on the door. But she wasn't home.

How could she not be home? It was Friday—she didn't have class. Suddenly he flushed again—she was probably off with Bump-Ass, that's where she was, ki—

Calm down, Secret Agent 666. I know where she is.

You do, Secret Agent 666?

I do, Sherlock: she's at school.

Of course she was at school; it was only 11:30 in the morning. Well, he would just have to free that bird. He put his hand in his pocket, remembered he had thrown out his cell after the disastrous call to Lenny, and went off to find a pay phone.

"Josiah Quincy Junior High."

It was amazing just how much boredom and unfriendliness could be crammed into those four words.

"Hello," said Alan, trying to speak as if in a great hurry. "I'm trying to get a message to a student, Juliet Jones. She forgot she has a dentist appointment today. Her mother will pick her up in the parking lot at noon."

And here she was, not ten minutes later, flying into the parking lot on those long, sure legs, the ends of her pink scarf fluttering behind her. When she saw Alan, she slowed to a walk, and then stood still. Then she turned around and started striding up the hill again. Alan sprang after her.

"Juliet! Stop!"

"Leave me alone!" she called over her shoulder. "You're not going to make me cut school."

"*Please*, Juliet . . ." he begged, touching her arm. "I really need you."

"You do?" she asked, turning back to him. "You're not just trying to get me in trouble?"

"No," he said simply. "I just need you."

"*Oh*," she said, and for a moment, the tears welled up in her beautiful brown eyes. "I needed to hear that."

"It's true," he assured her. And then: "So are you coming?"

"Coming?" she repeated stupidly. "Coming where?"

This time he was enough in control to swallow what he had been about to suggest. Obviously she was not yet ready to hear the truth about Lenny and the Boss. The last thing he needed was for her to think he was crazy.

"Uh—with me," he said. "Wherever. Let's just get out of here."

"All right," she said, sniffling. "I could stand to get out of here."

They walked together side by side across the field. Though her hand did not brush his, the wind kept picking up her pink scarf and tickling Alan's cheek with it.

"Sorry," she said, tucking the ends of it into her coat for the third time.

"Don't worry about it," he told her huskily. It was good to smell that Wisk smell again; he had not realized how much he'd missed it. It felt very good to be all alone with Juliet in the middle of an empty world.

"Where are we going?" she asked.

It was a strange question. Ten minutes before, he'd needed her help in the culvert more than anything, but she'd already made him forget.

"Right," he said, "to the culvert."

"Alan," she said severely. "I don't think you should be spending quite so much time in the culvert. You need a new game." She paused. "You know they all think you've gone mental, don't you?"

"Who?"

"Everyone. People who know you. People who don't know you. You seem different, you know—you're not the same as you used to be."

He flushed. "Well, what's wrong with that? You were always telling me I should change, before. Maybe I care about something now."

"Yeah, but Alan—I meant you were supposed to care about real things, like people, like art, and justice, and things like that."

"But I do, I do," he told her. "Isn't caring about Fordham caring about a person? Isn't keeping her safe caring about justice?"

"Just forget it," she said. "Let's go to my house."

It was just about the only place she could have suggested that he couldn't argue with. Her house! Her *house!* Her house in the middle of the day! It *must* mean something. His heart quickened in his throat, and the words of the Psalm they had read at his mother's funeral came back to him: *The mountains skipped like rams, the hills like lambs.* That's what it felt like, his heart skipping in his chest.

She opened the door and let him in, flipping on the lights in the kitchen. It was a small kitchen, a little cluttered, with a counter that separated it from the dining room beyond. Juliet threw her things on the counter and slipped her heavy boots off her long feet. Unconsciously, she laid her fingers on the counter as if it were a barre, pointed her left foot, and struck a quick beat against her right calf. Alan smiled. It was like peering into a little window into her life, seeing her do that so automatically. This is what she did in the afternoons. She came in, threw her things down on the Formica, did a quick dance move, and then she was home.

"I want to see you dance again," he told her. What was happening with his voice? It was all thick and husky; he seemed to have to work to remember to breathe.

"Well, you could come to my recital."

"What are you reciting?"

"My *dance* recital, you ignoramus! Next Friday. But you wouldn't want to come."

"Of course I'm coming."

"Really?" she cried. "Really, Alan? Because that would totally mean a lot to me, I—"

"Of course I'll be there," he said, more emphatically.

"Well, then," she said. "I guess I'll make you lunch."

They sat at the kitchen table, talking and not talking. It was so perfect that of course he had to go and ruin it. This time it was the troops who took it into their own heads to lead the charge. He watched them go in despair. *Come back, come back!* he called out to them in his head, but they were off: the suicide charge of the Light Brigade, just like the Tennyson poem Mrs. Perry had read to them:

> *"Forward, the Light Brigade!"*
> *Was there a man dismayed?*
> *Not tho' the soldier knew*
>   *Someone had blundered.*

Theirs not to make reply,
Theirs not to reason why,
Theirs but to do and die.
Into the valley of Death
  Rode the six hundred.

But six hundred soldiers were too many for Alan to stop; he could not call them back once they began pouring down the hill.

"I really missed you," the six hundred said huskily. Alan stood at the top of valley, waving for them to retreat: didn't they see this could only end in bloodshed?

"I missed you, too," Juliet muttered, so tenderly that hope surged in his chest. She laid her warm hand on his, and the six hundred luxuriated in their triumph. "See, this is what I was saying. I thought I'd lost you, and I can't *stand* losing you."

For a moment, in his magnanimous happiness, he almost felt sad for Connor Bumpass. The six hundred were celebrating; it was quite another poem he needed now to express his mood. And then she had to go and ruin it.

"So this is why we shouldn't go out. I can't handle fighting with you—"

Ambush! Ambush! In one horrible moment of massacre, the six hundred were slain. The few survivors lay twitching in their slow death throes.

She saw it in his face.

"Now you're angry," she cried unhappily. "I didn't want you to be angry, Alan, I . . ."

"Well, what if *I* don't want to be friends?" he interrupted her. "What if I only want to be friends if we go out with each other?"

"But I care too much about being friends with you to mess it up! I care about you *too much*—you have to believe me."

There is something about being presented with an illogical argument that can raise the blood pressure of a dead man.

"That's the stupidest thing I ever heard," Alan sputtered. "What, you'll only go out with guys you don't care about? So you don't care about Connor Bump-ass after all?"

"If you're going to insult him . . ." She stood.

It was ridiculous how much this hurt.

"I'm sorry, I'm sorry," he amended, "but Juliet . . . didn't you say you liked me more than you liked him?"

"This is stupid."

"Just tell me! Do you like Connor Bumpass more than you like me?"

"*This* is what I'm saying! I don't want to hurt you. . . ."

"I'd like to see what you do when you *do* want to hurt me," he cried out in his anguish. He stood up suddenly, as if propelled by the fire raging in his chest. He found his shoes and headed for the door.

"I gotta go," he said.

"All right," she said miserably. "So I guess I won't be seeing you at the recital."

"I'll be there!" he shouted at her. "I told you I would! Save me a seat right next to the Ass-bump." Then he raced down the street. The only thing he could think of was that he wanted to find something to punch, the harder the better.

T HAT NIGHT IN BED he realized it was a good thing that Juliet had rejected him. He had allowed her to distract him, and too many people were relying on him for that. He had to stay away from her, because the eighteenth was coming and he still didn't have a plan. He could go to the police, of course, but why bother, when they would just dismiss him as a crackpot? He could go to Trish, but she would just try to soothe him with stories of eccentric astronomers. He could go to Alice, but he knew what she would say. He had run into her that afternoon and had no desire to repeat the experience.

"Alan," she'd said, when she'd stopped him on the street. "I know we're not friends like we once were, but would you mind if I said something honest to you?"

"Sure," he'd said, looking longingly towards the crosswalk and to the freedom of being somewhere far, far away.

"It's just that you've been acting a little . . . *kooky*—and

I was just wondering if everything was all right at home, and if, you know, I could help."

"*Kooky?*" Alan had echoed. "So now I'm acting *kooky?*"

Alice had looked at him for a moment, sniffed, and tossed her head. "Never mind. I knew you'd get like this."

"What, *kooky?*"

"Forget it, Alan. I was just trying to help." And she left him standing there on the side of the road.

Now he rolled over and stared at the ceiling. The rough plaster had been spread on in a shell pattern that looked like waves; he saw himself like a lonely craft tossing on those swelling seas. It was clear that if anyone was going to save Governor Fordham and Lenny the thug, it would have to be Alan Green, acting alone.

But how was he going to do it? He could wait for them in the culvert on the night of the eighteenth, and then— then what? Rush at them with a pistol or whack 'em with a nightstick? It was, as they say, to laugh. Alan Green was a spy, not a solider. Fighting just wasn't his forte (and this he pronounced "fort" as Mrs. Perry had taught him, looking down on those who used the common but incorrect "fort-ay"). *Focus! Focus!* he screamed at himself. Governor Fordham was going to die as Alan stood around fumbling, letting himself get distracted by girls and vocabulary words.

What he needed was proof. If he could just show someone, but how . . . ? Suddenly, he sat up. That was it! He could use the video camera, that neglected birthday camera he had abandoned when he realized he would never be another Hitchcock. He slipped from his bed and padded through his bathroom to the other room. The camera was there, somewhere, hidden away by the unfeeling maid who tidied things away with no thought as to whether Alan would be able to find them again. But, ah, there it was, stashed behind some tapes. He picked it up, snapping it on.

So now what? he asked himself in the strange dark of his midnight room.

We take a leaf from the enemy, he told himself. *We lay a trap.*

But then: *Won't it be too dark to film anything at night?*

This was a stopper. He was not sure if there would be enough light, and in the middle of that sleepless night, it felt that knowing *right then* was akin to taking a stand against the Boss. Silently, he dressed in double layers, and then he retrieved the hideous ski parka that he had banished to his closet. He needed something else, too—where was it, that sleeping bag he'd wheedled Trish into buying before he'd realized camping was boring? He found it under the couch in his other room, and then, silently, he crept down the servants' stairs and out the door.

He had never been outside that late. Pale shadows from the moon gave everything an odd, underwater look as Alan skulked along in the spiky shade of the leafless trees. It was strange how awake he felt, how alive, now that he had a purpose. He took deep, bracing breaths of the frosty air. Somewhere, that night, Lenny was laying his plan for the governor; somewhere, that night, the Boss was laying his plan for Lenny; and here was Alan, laying his plan for the Boss. There was a kind of symmetry to that: wheels within wheels.

The bridge's one streetlamp buzzed and came on as Alan reached the culvert, and then buzzed and went off again. Alan swore. The dim light from the police station next door was no help to his camera, either—he would have to trust the streetlight, and that was dodgy. There was also the problem of where to hide—the bridge was too exposed to offer any sort of blind. Alan imagined them coming, the Boss pulling his white car off to the side, Lenny dragging his game leg behind as he limped to his doom. They would see him right away, unless he was in the culvert, and if he was in the culvert, he wouldn't catch anything on film. Or—well, that must be it. He'd have to use the car. He'd just have to hide there in the culvert and wait until the car came, and then he could creep out and train his camera on the handoff.

He practiced creeping up from his hiding place, crouching down stealthily behind hypothetical cars, and then, nearly satisfied, he retreated back into the culvert and imagined what it would be like waiting there during the stakeout. It wasn't too bad, actually, inside his dorky coat and the dorky sleeping bag—he could wait for the Boss all night, if he needed to. A snuffling sound startled him then, and he looked over and saw an opossum in the mouth of the culvert, blinking in surprise as he saw that Alan had invaded his territory. It was a strange reminder,

Alan felt, of how much of the creation did not give a rat's ass about Alan and Fordham and the rest of humanity's problems—but Alan was not an opossum, and he cared. He shooed it away and went back to his vigil.

It was the first time he had spent the whole night awake. It was a strange feeling, passing so many hours without moving or making a sound, not being sure whether he was thinking of dreaming or dreaming of thinking. But then it was morning, and the birds were chattering away. Alan crawled out of his cave to see the dawn. It was very disappointing to see how unspectacular the eastern sky was—it was a total gyp, he felt, that dawn was so dull compared to sunset. He yawned. The new sun was casting spiky shadows from the grass on the concrete sides of the culvert, and for a moment, they looked to Alan like tall thin warriors bobbing and praying as they went off to war. He was like that, especially when he was tired—he saw things in inanimate objects—not in a crazy way, of course, but the way you might see faces in rest-room fixtures (the faucet a nose, the hot and cold handles the eyes). Or doorstops—those reminded him of deer, with the screws like eyes and the black rubber tips like noses—those were the sort of things he saw. Now he found himself slipping the camera from its case and filming the grass soldiers.

Why are you doing this? he asked himself. *You should be thinking about Fordham, not this artsy crap.*

But it makes me happy, he answered. *Don't I deserve a little of that?*

He didn't answer himself. After a while he got up and went home. He slept until noon.

It was funny, now that he had planned his trap, how much he wished that the eighteenth would just hurry up and come. The weight of expectation seemed to crush him, and the image of Fordham haunted him in his quiet moments. Whenever he closed his eyes at night or in the low moments of Spanish class, he unwillingly saw the governor going about her last oblivious moments. He imagined her getting into her car and cursing the traffic, not knowing that those moments she was wasting were the last moments she had on earth.

Sometimes he would see her opening the car door and throwing her beat-up leather portfolio down onto the passenger's seat, and then he would know he wasn't thinking about the governor so much as about his mother. He hated it. He had spent two years trying not to think about that day, and now he found he couldn't stop himself. He saw her chucking her portfolio onto the other crap on the passenger's seat and obliviously starting the car. From the expression on her face, he knew she thought it was going to be a trip like any other. But it wasn't going to be a trip like any other, and it really bothered him that she hadn't known that. She hadn't known she didn't need to bother with the dry cleaning; she hadn't known she could have treated herself to a giant banana split with nuts and whipped cream without having to worry about getting fat; she hadn't even known to say a special good-bye to her son.

He put his face in his hands. He didn't want to be thinking any of this, but he couldn't stop wondering how she would have lived her life differently if she had known she would only get thirty-five years on earth. Would she have crammed more into them? Would she have climbed Mount Everest, or written great poems, or found cures for malaria? Would she have finally found her calling that would have made her life meaningful? Or was it just an illusion that there could be any meaning to life at all? Certainly the opossums didn't care what silly things human beings did with their lives—but then again, Alan cared. He cared a lot, and he knew in his heart that there had been some meaning in his mother's life at least, because he missed her so damn much now that she was gone.

Here was the sick thing of it: he almost looked forward to talking this over with Kellerman. He really hated Kellerman, hated the way that the most offhand comment could set him off nodding like a bobblehead dashboard doll of Sigmund Freud, but all that weekend and through the insufferable grind of the next week, he found himself thinking about Kellerman's office with something akin to anticipation. It was some sort of psychosis, he guessed, that made it impossible to hate somebody thoroughly once you spent some time with them. He guessed that if he were locked in solitary confinement with Rory Frankel, he might even get to like that bastard—which showed that he was already beginning to lose it. How could he be in solitary confinement with another person? His brain was beginning to go.

Luckily, Kellerman chose the next Thursday to be so irritating that even Alan in his psychotic state couldn't feel affectionate towards him.

"I notice that your report card is rather spotty this first semester," Kellerman said, holding a printout close to his face. Alan shrugged.

"Mrs. Perry seems to find your work quite brilliant," Kellerman went on, "and yet in your other classes—even your writing classes—your work is universally described as not rising up to your potential."

Alan shrugged again. He was staring at the smug, smiling visage of Connor Bumpass in the basketball picture.

"I believe education is very important to your father, is it not?"

Alan shrugged. "Sure."

"Do you think it's possible you are purposefully trying to disappoint your father by not trying to reach your full potential?"

This was not only stupid, but maddeningly illogical.

"Why couldn't I just disappoint him by not trying at all?"

"Ah," Kellerman said, with a "now we're getting some-where" look on his face. "And why do you think you want to disappoint him?"

"Are you sure you have a Ph.D.?" asked Alan. "You seem like you're kind of missing the point."

"Am I?" *Bobble bobble bobble.* It sometimes amazed Alan that Kellerman got paid for this crap. "Well, maybe we should talk about something that interests *you.* Why don't you tell me what your spy group has been discover-ing lately?"

For a second Alan could barely breathe. At last he man-aged an inadequate *"What!"*

"Your spy group. You remember—the one you were telling me about, with the cigarettes."

This was just outrageous.

"It's just a stupid game—" Alan blustered.

"This . . . *stupid game,* as you call it, seems to be taking up quite a lot of your time."

"Says who?"

"Says your father. He called me. He's *worried,* Alan. He says you spend all your time wandering about alone and using your computer to write up stories of gruesome assassinations and gravel left in the shape of messages in Braille." Kellerman leaned back in his chair and let the bombshell fall.

For a moment, the force of the bomb knocked the wind out of Alan's lungs. *This is it,* he thought wildly. *Every-thing that doesn't make me stronger is going to kill me.*

"How did he know that?" he asked when he was in

charge of his breath again. "Did he go into my computer? How dare he . . ."

Kellerman let him go on and on, and then he said: "It does show he cares, doesn't it?"

"Who cares if he cares? I don't *care* if he cares—I just want him out of my goddamn stuff!"

"*I* care that he cares," Kellerman said in his annoying reasonable voice. "And I must say your . . . *spy work* sounds very inventive."

"It's just a stupid game," Alan spat. It was a betrayal of all he held dear, saying that, but then again, this was war. When he finally managed to squirm out of Kellerman's clutches, he spoke in his head to Roberta Bismo. *I didn't mean any of it*, he said. *You know how it is. Just give your name, rank, and serial number. That's all I gave.*

He was still reeling from the blow when he staggered out of Kellerman's office, but there was another enemy lurking there. He had successfully avoided Juliet all week, ignoring her calls, slipping into empty classrooms when he saw her approaching, but now she was waiting to ambush him in the hall. Well, he was wily, he would not be trapped. He turned on his heel and walked away from her, even as she called out his name.

Finally, she grabbed his shoulder. "Alan," she said, "listen—about last week—I'm so sorry. I've been trying to say I'm sorry all week, and to ask you . . . ." She looked a little puffy, as if she'd been crying. "Please, Alan, can't you be the way you were before? I really need you to be the way you used to be."

"No," he told her. "I can't. I can't let you distract me. I have other things to worry about now."

"Other things?" she sniffed. "What other things?"

He stiffened. *"Things,"* he said testily.

She threw up her hands. "You're not talking about the governor, are you? I'm talking about a *real* problem you could help me with, and you're talking about that stupid *game!*"

She was almost crying, but Alan steeled his resolve. He would not be distracted.

"Is it life or death?" he asked her.

"What!"

"This problem you're talking about—is it life or death? Because if it's not, it'll have to wait until after the eighteenth, because until then I'm kind of busy. . . ."

"After the eighteenth?" she repeated wildly, and her tears seemed to freeze in the chill that descended on her.

"Yeah," he said. "I'm going to try and stop them on the eighteenth." He snuck a look at her. She was so quiet now he almost felt she was about to disappear. He softened. "You could come and help," he told her.

"I'm going to be busy on the eighteenth," she informed him coldly. "I told you. That's my *recital*. Oh, I *knew* you weren't coming!" She took a deep breath and blinked twice before turning away from him. "I never really thought you would come, anyway."

This hurt him to the quick. "I would, I would," he told her, "I really would, if two lives weren't at stake. . . ."

"Whatever," she said. She slung her shoe bag over her shoulder, and then she was gone.

▼

IT WAS WEDNESDAY AFTERNOON, the sixteenth of December, and Alan stood at a pay phone, hesitating, waffling, *vacillating.* When you came down to it, the whole problem was that he was a coward. He could not stand up and accept the humiliation of trying to save Fordham's life—he had to do it crouching in the anonymity of a phone booth. At last he dialed.

"Governor Fordham's office."

"Listen," whispered Alan furtively. "I'm not trying to make a threat or anything—this is more of a warning. I'm really worried there's going to be another attack on the governor on Saturday. And you might want to check out the owner of a white Ford Probe, Massachusetts license plate CPR 1."

"Why? Who is this?"

"Just tell her to be careful, okay?"

And he beat it out of there before they could trace the call.

The blood was pounding in his ears and half-formed plans were flying before his eyes as he walked home, so that he almost banged into Morris Kaufman on the far side of the Center. It was symptomatic of his preoccupation that he didn't run away, but let himself get drawn into conversation with the loser, who kept doing stupid little feints and jabs and karate moves seen in the worst sort of Saturday-morning movies. When he saw Alan he feinted and jabbed once again and executed a clumsy roundhouse kick that just managed to get Alan in the kidneys.

"What the hell are you doing?" Alan demanded, rubbing his back. "I tell you, Kaufman, there are times . . ."

Kaufman wilted. "There are times, what?" he bleated.

Well, maybe this was the time for brutal honesty. "It's just this," said Alan impatiently. "Don't you ever wonder why it's *you* Frankel's always after?"

"No," Kaufman said, hanging his head. "I don't wonder about it at all."

This stopped Alan. If it had been him, he would have wondered; he would have railed against God as Job did in the Bible, the way he had when it was *his* mother who had been picked off by randomness. But Kaufman almost looked as if he accepted his outrageous fate. He stood there like a wilted flower in his stupid kung fu jacket with the limp yellow belt as if he felt he deserved it.

"You've got to be kidding me," groaned Alan. "What, don't you hate him? Don't you blame him?"

"Of course I hate him," Kaufman whispered.

"Yeah, but don't you *blame* him?" Alan pressed, and then, when Kaufman didn't answer: "Oh, *man*—you really do need help. Look, Kaufman, why don't you *do* something about it? Stand up to him! Fight for yourself! Show him you're a . . ."

The unspoken word hung there in the air.

"What? A man? A *mensch*?"

"Well, yeah!" said Alan. "Just fight back for once—show him you're not just some spineless idiot who accepts everything that's thrown at him. Don't *be* the sort of person who deserves Frankel pounding on him!"

"You really think so?" Kaufman cowered.

"God, yes."

"You think I should challenge him to a fight, or something?"

"I don't care how you do it. Just show him you're not dirt under his feet."

"Oh," said Kaufman. And then, "Thank you, Alan."

Alan didn't answer. He had already turned back to his own problems.

That night he dreamed about Alice. It was funny how much the dream made him want to talk to her, to hear her attack the Fordham problem with all her incisive intelligence. He imagined how he could explain it to her: *It's not that I don't think the SRU used to be a joke, Al, but it's just like Pluto. It was the wrong analysis that led me to a real*

threat. And the threat is really really real, and it's going to happen really soon.

He needed her. He went to school early and sat on the big rock to wait. And there she was, striding through the unfriendly crowds so easily, Agnes following behind, hunching her shoulders against the unfriendliness there as if against a biting wind. Alan stood up and began to walk towards them, but suddenly he lost his nerve. He couldn't stand there and hear Alice tell him he was a *kooky*, unfeeling bastard, not now, not when he needed her so much. He went back to the rock and laid his head on his knees.

God, he was so alone! They say that every point in the universe is rushing away from every other at unimaginable speeds, and here was the proof of it. At every moment, Alan felt more and more alone, exiled to Pluto to spin alone in the growing darkness. He watched Alice and Agnes orbiting each other like some contained binary system; he watched Juliet, beautiful Juliet, sailing farther and farther away on her trajectory towards Connor Bumpass while Alan hugged his knees and floated lonely in space.

Help me, he begged the universe. *Let me find someone to help me save the governor. I can't do it alone.*

He couldn't do it alone. He needed someone and he couldn't afford to be picky. And there was Keith Reese, surrounded by a knot of other kids. Sticking his pride into his back pocket, Alan went up to them.

"So I was just wondering," he said, trying to summon up all the cool detachment he had taken for granted three months before. "What are you doing Friday night?"

Keith's nose was twitching as if something smelled bad. Suddenly Alan wanted to puke. It was the stench of losers Keith smelled, and the loser he smelled was Charles Alan Green. *Don't ask for whom the smell tolls,* he told himself. *That smell tolls for thee.*

"I'm kinda busy," said Keith, his fat lip rolling into the faintest of sneers. "I have rehearsal."

"Rehearsal?"

Rehearsal. In Alan's absence, it seemed, Keith had somehow tumbled into the lead in *Carousel,* and now these kids—these *actors*—were his new friends. "So you see," he told Alan, "I don't really have time anymore for you and your little games."

Well, screw you, Keith! Alan screamed in his head as the troupe moved away. *I guess you always were a pretty good actor—I could have sworn you were my friend.* But the situation was growing desperate—he didn't have time to dwell on Keith. He needed someone else—anyone would do.

"Hey! Jethro!"

Stupid little Jethro: he would come. He had always been one of the outer planets to Alan's sun—Pluto, really—and he would be sure to fall back into Alan's gravitational pull when he called. True, he was annoying in large doses, but one night with Jethro during a stakeout wouldn't kill him. "Hey, Jethro! What are you doing Friday night?"

Jethro turned, and the girl who stood next to him turned, too, walking around him in a circle as if she were an extension of his arm. It was Megan Henderson, and she and Jethro were joined at the hands like some sort of weird experiment on the Island of Dr. Moreau. Megan Henderson! How could she be walking down the halls publicly holding hands with Jethro? It just made no sense—Alan hadn't been gone *that* long.

I'm like Rip Van goddamn Winkle, he thought, feeling his chin to make sure no beard had somehow sprouted there. *I've woken up in some goddamn alternative universe.*

Just in case they still spoke English in whatever strange universe he had found himself in, he spoke to them. "Hey, Megan—hey, Jethro, I was just wondering—what are you doing Friday?"

The strange two-headed Siamese Beast that was Jethro and Megan inclined its two heads inward and exchanged a secret, loving glance.

"We're like kind of busy," boasted the Jethro-Head.

"We're *always* busy," giggled the Megan-Head, and then the two of them dissolved back into a world where no one else existed. Alan beat it. He sure as hell wasn't going to linger in *that* alternate universe; even the terrible one where he found himself responsible for Lenny and Governor Fordham's safety seemed better than the cooing of that two-headed beast.

"*You're* so cute."

"No, *you're* so cute."

Really, it was enough to make you want to puke. And it

meant that if anyone was going to save Governor Fordham, it was going to be Alan alone.

And then, in the middle of English class, he suddenly realized how he could get Juliet to come. He could do something for her, show her that he wasn't as unfeeling as she thought. He could go to her recital.

But what about the trap?

I'll set up everything before. Besides, I only have to go for a little while—just long enough to show her I'm not a bastard.

The next night, promptly at seven, Secret Agent 666 slunk into the high school auditorium. Moments later he realized what he had done: this recital was not the Juliet Jones show. First he had to endure the torture of watching twenty-seven small girls in pink tutus walk across the stage to the tuneless plonking of a dilapidated piano—neither dancers nor piano, it seemed, had been introduced to the concept of rhythm. Alan slouched down in his broken seat. In the old Soviet Union, he thought, such lackluster performers would have been taken out and shot.

Painfully, he suffered through the sight of twenty-seven older girls, in blue tutus this time, turning around to a tune vaguely reminiscent of *The Nutcracker*. This act, at least, provided the amusement of an unchoreographed collision. The acts dragged on and on; Alan sank farther and farther into his seat. When would Juliet get on? He counted hats; he navigated the cracks on the ceiling. His mind flew back to the culvert, and to the transaction that might be happening there, even now. Even now, *now*, Lenny could be shuffling through the leaves towards the Boss to hand him whatever proof it was that he had done his part. Then the Boss would bring out his Lugar and . . . Alan struggled up. He'd let himself get distracted again, in his weakness. His place was in the culvert, not here. He struggled to stand up, to force his shaking arms into his coat, but then he saw her: Juliet was alone on the stage.

Hisses came from behind that he should sit down. Alan sat. He sat and watched, amazed. Even if the Boss had appeared at the back of the room and announced his intention to shoot Governor Fordham right then and there, Alan would have had to sit and watch. Because Juliet was extraordinary. There was a quality to her dancing that made her seem like an entirely different creature from the others. The others let their hands flop around like fish, but Juliet looked as if every inch of her was liquid steel, and she offered up her limbs with a grace and generosity the others never could have achieved. Her slender arms were held before her as she walked with indescribable loveliness on the tips of her toes, and Alan almost thought he could see a giant invisible ball held there in her arms. Then, flat-footed, she leaned backwards; she leaned backwards so far that any normal human being would have fallen over. But Juliet did not fall; the liquid steel that had been in her arms somehow settled into her planted feet, and nothing could disrupt her. Alan nearly choked on his heart in his throat. He was torn between terror that she would fall and the beautiful impossibility of her being able to hold that position, and then she was up again, rising up on her toes, arms grasping the invisible ball; she was dancing with the invisible ball.

When the tremendous applause came crashing down, Alan looked around again for Connor Bumpass. How could Bumpass stand it? Why wasn't he rushing up onto the stage to capture that indescribable beauty in his arms? But Bumpass didn't seem to be there at all. Alan burned with sudden indignation. How dare he miss this, when it meant so much to Juliet? He had always been planning to slink away before he saw Connor Bumpass appear to claim her, but now he pushed through the crowd to where she was coming out a side door. He stood before her, mouth agape.

"Holy crap," he said finally.

Juliet raised an eyebrow. "Alan Green," she said, "meet my parents."

Alan flushed as he tried to shake their hands. *Holy crap? Holy crap!* He tried blinking to dislodge the echoes of his stupid words out of his ears, and then, thinking how he probably looked like some victim of Tourette's syndrome, twitching and blinking and cursing inappropriately, he blushed harder.

"You were *unbelievable*," he said to her. "I can't *believe* how good you were." He had not been able to take his eyes off her since she had emerged from the side door. He was quite positive now she was the most beautiful girl he had ever seen.

"Thanks," she said. Her eyes met his, and suddenly the aloof look she had worn like a pair of sunglasses since she had seen him standing there disappeared. Her brow knitted, and one of her eyes suddenly shone as if she were holding back tears.

"You really liked it," she said.

It was as if everyone else fell away when she looked at him with those eyes.

"Holy crap," he said again.

He walked back to her house with her parents, thinking about her dance. The memory of her dancing, of holding the invisible ball as she walked impossibly on the tips of her toes, the leaning back: it almost hurt him that he couldn't see it again. It was like a gaping wound, that memory. Juliet and her parents chatted about this and that, and Alan trailed behind them, wondering where Connor Bumpass had been.

When they reached her house, Juliet's parents invited Alan in, plying him with soda and cookies. Then they retired to another part of the house, and Alan and Juliet were alone.

"Where was Bumpass?" Alan choked out.

Juliet looked the other way. "I told him not to come," she said. "Not that he would have, anyway. We broke up last week."

"Last week?" Alan echoed.

"Yeah. Turns out he's kind of an idiot."

She still hadn't looked at him.

"Why didn't you tell me?"

"I tried to tell you," she said. "I tried to tell you that day in front of Kellerman's office, but you were so strange, and you said you cared more about the game than me, and . . ."

The game—holy crap again! How was it possible that he had forgotten? He suddenly thought of Governor Fordham, and his heart froze.

"I forgot," he said wonderingly. "You made me forget. I was going to go there right after . . ."

Juliet started to say something, and then she stopped.

"You're really worried," she said, and it was like she was understanding him for the first time. "You're *really* worried. Alan—Charles—it's not just a game for you, is it? You really care."

He couldn't answer; he could only nod.

"Well," she said, "if you care that much, I guess I should trust you. Come on. Let's go to the culvert."

It had rained, and the sides of the embankment were icy. They skidded down, clutching each other. The half-light of the moon cast a gray and eerie light on the frosted leaves, and Alan and Juliet huddled together in the dark. No one was out. If the Boss had not already sprung his trap, he would have apparent privacy when he met Lenny on the bridge.

But when they heard the footsteps coming, it was not Lenny's familiar shuffling gait—they were lighter footsteps, footsteps that stopped now and again, as if someone were stopping to kick at an invisible opponent. Alan put his fingers to his lips and crept silently up to the edge. When he saw what was there, he swore.

There was Kaufman, his kung fu bathrobe peeking out from under his parka. He was feinting and jabbing with all the ferocity of a rabbit, and coming up the road to meet him was Rory Frankel with three of his thugs.

"Oh, no," Alan moaned. "Not like this, you idiot!"

"What's happening?" Juliet hissed.

"It's Kaufman trying to show he's a man," Alan groaned. "But he's going to be a *dead* man if he doesn't run. Run, Kaufman, you moron!"

Up above, they could hear Kaufman making his futile last stand.

"I'm here to settle this, Frankel," Kaufman said, in a voice as weedy and as pencil-necked as his body. Rory Frankel and his thugs all laughed then, and Alan knew that the coming massacre was all his fault.

I need to do something, he thought. *I know—I'll film it.* But the camera was still at home, where he had planned to get it after the recital. His eyes flew to the police station, just three hundred feet away—but Frankel would see him if he left the cover of the culvert. *Call them!* he thought. Instinctively, his hand went to his pocket before he remembered he had thrown the phone away. But hold on—he had thrown the phone away here, *here* in the culvert, as if the universe had wanted him to have it for just this moment. He tore through the leaves, looking for it, as the fates pulled Morris Kaufman inexorably towards his destruction. His hand hit something hard, but it was only a rock.

"You want to settle this, you turd?" Frankel mocked. "All right, we'll settle it." And even as Alan's hand felt the phone at last, he heard the sound of Frankel fist hitting Kaufman flesh.

Alan was still fumbling with the phone when he saw Juliet pour out of the culvert like a panther. His hand went out to grab her, to stop her, to save her, but she was racing like liquid steel up the steep embankment towards Kaufman. Terrified, he followed, and he saw her towering form between Kaufman and his tormentors. She seemed a hundred feet tall in the intermittent glow of the flickering streetlight, standing like an angel of vengeance over the crouched bullies. There was a fire in her eyes, an anger in her curling lip—it was as if her skin had been stripped away so that it showed passion beneath. Alan felt again what he had felt when he'd seen her dancing—the longing, the desire to be like her, if just a little bit, and yes, the love of her, the love of her rightness—she was towering over the bullies, spitting in her fury, and she was glorious.

"You stop that!" she commanded, her voice rolling over them like thunder. "What sort of disgusting, cowardly people are you, to attack Morris like that? Are you *proud* of yourselves? Are you so stupid and pathetic that *this* is all you can think to do with your lives? Do you think anyone will ever admire you? Is *this* all you have to make your life worth living? You leave this boy alone *right now!*"

Amazingly, they were cowed; for a moment Alan thought they might run away. But they were approaching Juliet again, the four of them, like hyenas slinking towards a lion in the flickering light.

"Oh, look," Frankel said, falling back on what served him for wits. "It's Ballerina Juliet!" And he did a little movement that was supposed to be some sort of dance step.

"Tease away," said Juliet in that terrible calm voice. "It won't improve my opinion of you."

"She's so *mature*," Frankel said to the others. "It must be the ballet." And he did another stupid leap. Or maybe it wasn't so stupid. The leap brought him closer, and in a horrible flash Alan saw what he was going to do. Frankel couldn't scare her, but he could hurt her, and he could hurt her where it would hurt her dancing. He would go for the legs, go for the feet. Alan could see it all, hear the big ugly steel-toed boot thwak against her shin, but before steel hit bone, he had thrown the cell phone away and was racing up to protect her, to save her—in a moment he was standing at her side on the road over Kaufman.

Kaufman lay on the ground, very still, twin rivulets of blood coming out of his broken nose. He was a pathetic thing, limp, pale, very ugly, so very dorky it made Alan cringe, but at the same time the sight of him released a kaleidoscope of fear and anger, setting loose thoughts of death and vengeance, and a desperate hatred for the sadism of Rory Frankel and of CRAP. How dare they! How dare they inflict their misery on a miserable world! A righteous anger came over him, and he rushed at Frankel, screaming like a berzerker.

"Get off him!" he shouted. "Just get the hell off him!"

Frankel laughed; he put up his hands in a gesture of warding off a crazy person. "Keep your skirt on," he said, looking at his goons with a twirling finger to the temple to tell them, as if it were not obvious, that Alan Green was crazy. "Come on, Green, I thought you were cool. Why do you give a crap about this homo?"

"Because!" Alan shouted, the blood pounding in his ears like the beat of martial drums. How could he explain it? Because Kaufman was a person, because he had a heart and brain and twoeyestwoarmstwolegs, he was a person, just like Alan, and he was suffering, and that was reason enough. "Because!" he shouted again. It was ridiculous, what he said next, *humiliating*, *mortifying*, and yet at same time the truest thing he had ever said, the words of John Donne falling out of his babbling mouth, without him knowing what he was going to say: "Because any man's death diminishes me, because I am involved in mankind!"

It was true. He knew it was true, and for a moment he felt strangely expanded, larger than himself, part of the great well of stupid, sniveling, glorious humanity, and he knew he had to defend stupid, sniveling, glorious humanity the best he could. The six hundred were set forth again, and they hit Frankel full-on with the force of fury.

The two of them went down into the street, rolling on the pavement, with much grunting and swearing, and it was a long moment before Alan was sure which arms and legs were his. He was grappling with his enemy, holding him down, and with all his might he wished he could free his hand and sock Rory Frankel right in the face, pound at him with all the fear and fury he'd felt ever since the first time he'd seen Kaufman slammed up against the lockers. But it wasn't happening the way he wanted, not at all. Instead, it was Frankel who had his hand free, and Alan who was flat on his back, staring up into the dark and the light rain as Frankel's steel-toed fist slammed into his nose.

How had it happened? He had done the right thing, hadn't he? Hadn't he for once in his life done the good thing, the noble thing, in rushing out to save Juliet and that idiot of a Kaufman? And where were the angels from heaven swooping down to save him? His head hit the pavement again, releasing a spray of stars and a dull throbbing ache, and a boot slammed into his ribs. His bleary eyes flew up to the flag that snapped in the rain right above the police station, hoping for some succor there, and he cursed himself again for having thrown the phone away. *God! God!* he cried as another shoe smashed into his side, but no angel came running, not even in the lumpy form of Kellerman, running down the side of the hill, ugly brown coat flapping about him like the wings of some demented bird. But the boot had paused in its awful rhythm, and as Alan looked up through the slanting rain, he saw Juliet, her arms wrapped around Frankel's neck, wrestling him off Alan, and that was as close to an angel as he was going to get.

He closed his eyes then, so he did not see the moment the police arrived, having guessed from Alan's abortive phone call and the sounds out their windows where the trouble was. Juliet and Kaufman and Frankel and the rest of the goons they took to juvenile detention, but they took one look at the bloody mess that had so recently been Alan Green, and him they brought to the emergency room.

I N THE HOSPITAL, they thought he was delirious.

"It's the concussion," they told his father as he sat by Alan's bed in the emergency room. His father's face looked pale and worried, not at all like the time Keith had shot him, when his father had yelled and called him a goddamn idiot. Now Alan kept his blackened eyes closed; it hurt to open them, anyway. It hurt to talk, too, but he had to. When he managed to get the humiliating scene of his John Donne quoting and his resulting pulverization out of his mind, he realized the scene on the bridge had been another distraction. He had forgotten his real work. The buzzing hands of the emergency-room clock jerked spasmodically in their relentless passage towards the nineteenth of December, and Alan still had to stop the Boss.

"Who's Erica?" they asked him, to get him to calm down, and when they heard as much of the story as Alan could get out through his swollen, rubbery lips, they laughed a little in relief, and said it was the concussion.

So they brought Alan and his concussion home, his broken ribs wrapped up in tape, and tucked him into bed with a cold drink and a long straw. Then they turned out the lights and closed the door, and left Erica Fordham to her fate, with only Alan to care about her.

Early on the morning of the nineteenth, Alan staggered to his feet and limped downstairs. His father stood up from the table, tousled Alan's hair as gently as he could, and marched him back up again. This dance was repeated several times. At last Trish came upstairs and sat on Alan's feet to keep him from moving.

"I have to go," he croaked at her. "No one believes me, so no one else can stop them. . . . It's going to happen at nine thirty-five. . . ."

"Alan," she said seriously. "You've been hit on the head. No head, not even one as thick as yours, is designed to be hit that hard. You have to believe us. *You need to be in bed.* Tomorrow you can go save the world."

"Tomorrow's too late," he protested feebly, but they must have slipped him a mickey in his orange juice, because he fell back asleep then and didn't wake up until the morning of the twentieth.

It was snowing when Alan woke up, a clean white snow that fell on the just and the unjust and on the garbage cans that lined the driveway. Alan sat with his throbbing head propped up against the window and looked out on its white purity. Lenny and Fordham were dead, and Kaufman, too, for all he knew, and CRAP and Frankel were free to ride roughshod over the world. There was no justice at all, he thought. In the end life was just what Shakespeare said, a tale told by an idiot, full of sound and fury, signifying nothing.

Trish came in with his breakfast on a tray.

"She's dead, isn't she?" he asked her dully.

"Who, Alan? Juliet? She's fine. She wasn't hurt at all. In fact, she's called you seven times already. Do you want me to bring you the phone . . . ?"

"Not *her*," Alan corrected. "The governor. They killed her yesterday, didn't they?"

Trish stared at him blankly.

"That's why I was there . . ." he started, but it was too hard to explain how he'd known. He just wanted to hear he was right and get it over with.

"Governor Fordham?" Trish repeated slowly. "Nothing happened to the governor—she's fine. Are you still thinking about that assassination attempt, Alan? Is this about that spy game you were playing?"

"It's not a game," he insisted. "It's not! They were planning to kill her yesterday! Something must have happened. . . ."

"So you weren't there to protect Morris?" Trish asked in surprise. "I thought you were there for him."

"God, no," Alan answered, closing his eyes.

"Oh," said Trish, and she paused. She sat down next to him, smoothing the wrinkles out of his blanket, and then she said, "But you *did* protect him. It was a very brave, very *noble* thing to do." She paused. "I really admire you for it."

Alan didn't answer, and then Trish began to laugh.

"What?" Alan said.

"Remember that story about Pluto I told you? How they found a planet because they were looking in the wrong place for something else?"

"Yeah."

"Well, maybe that's like you and Kaufman. Maybe you were out there to help Fordham, but Kaufman's your Pluto."

But Alan didn't want to think about that. He had a sudden flash of Juliet pulling Frankel off him as he blubbered on and on about being involved with mankind, and involuntarily, he shut his eyes. He was soft, just as she'd accused him of being, and he wasn't sure the memory of his weakness would ever let him see her again. The full force of his humiliation fell upon him, and he collapsed onto the pillows.

"Take me with you," he begged Trish. "When you go back to Cincinnati, will you please take me with you?"

Trish pressed his hand gently.

"Tell you what," she said. "I made a decision while you were getting patched up in the hospital. I think I'm going to stay a little longer, a few months more, maybe. I may be flattering myself, but I don't think you're quite ready for me to leave. Alan Green, don't you *dare* get sentimental on me—my weak heart can't stand the shock."

She leaned down and kissed him. "I do love you," she whispered into his hair. "But I promise not to say it too often. And Alan—"

"Yeah?"

"You do get to go to college in four and a half years."

■ + ■

Monday he was still too doped up to go to school. On Tuesday, he was better, but he didn't want to go.

"Why not?"

"I just don't want to."

"You have to go back sometime," his father started, but Cheryl laid her hand on his and he stopped.

"Of course he has to go back *sometime*, Mitch," she said, "but maybe not today."

So he didn't. He stayed in the clothes he'd been sleeping in for days, drank orange juice, and read the paper. He scoured the paper for clues; he combed the columns for some hint of what had gone awry with CRAP's plans. For Erica Fordham was undoubtedly alive, flush with the politically correct pleasures of the holiday season. The public preparations for Kwanzaa went on as planned; no snipers appeared at the menorah lighting on Tuesday.

And then, in the same way he had known with such certainty that Erica Fordham's life was in danger, Alan suddenly understood that he'd been an idiot, just as everyone else had already known. Of *course* he'd been wrong: it was plainly ridiculous to think that assassins would communi-

cate with one another through the iconography of cigarette packages or forge lovesick letters to lay out their
nefarious plans. Along with the humiliating memory of
writhing on the ground muttering "I am involved in
mankind!" it made him want to puke. He had never hated
himself quite so much before.

"Sink hairs," he said to the ceiling, gingerly feeling his
broken ribs. "It was all sink hairs. It meant nothing." And
it wasn't just CRAP that meant nothing—*everything*
meant nothing; he had broken his ribs for nothing. Here
he was, having done the noble thing for the first time in
his life, and for what? He'd had the crap well and truly
kicked out him. The old Alan might have tried to find
meaning in it, but this was a newer and wiser model.
Sound and fury, he said to himself again. *A tale told by an
idiot. I'm an idiot. But I won't be an idiot anymore. I'm not
looking for meaning, not ever again.*

And why had he been so bent on looking for meaning in
everything, anyway? His Jewish ancestors had had it right
as they suffered and died in the shtetl. The Christian part
of the Bible was all full of meaning and love and heaven
and crap, but the Old Testament told it like it is. It was
full of the grouchy reality that the race is not always to
the swift nor the battle to the strong (well, the battle
often went to the strong, but that was part of the problem). He remembered the reading at his mother's funeral
from the book of Job, where that poor schmuck had gone
to God to ask for meaning, and God had answered him
with the big old cosmic *nanny-nanny-boo-boo*, saying peo-

ple are just too small and stupid to get it—even if there's any meaning out there, it's not for us to know. Or it might be that Keith was right: maybe there was no meaning at all, and the best we could hope for was to find lessons in the senselessness. What had he learned from Frankel's fist exactly? Well, for starters, he'd learned that it really, really, *really* hurts to have the crap well and truly kicked out of you.

He dug his fists into his eyes. *I really am losing it*, he thought, and then he began to cry. It was the final straw of his humiliation, that he couldn't keep himself from crying. But he couldn't stop. He cried because he hurt and he cried because he had been such an idiot about CRAP and he cried because he had not been able to stop them from hurting Kaufman and he cried because he had not cried at his mother's funeral and he cried because he could not stop crying.

On Wednesday afternoon Trish came to his door.

"Juliet was here," she said.

"I don't want to see her."

"I know," she told him. "I told her you needed more time. But she gave me this."

This was a letter from Mrs. Perry. Alan read it after Trish left the room.

Dear Alan: the letter read, in her strict, no-nonsense, but infinitely gracious script.

I am very sorry to hear about what happened to you, and I trust that you are slowly recuperating and will eventually be bored enough to return to school. Something (well, someone who cares for you) tells me that you are very troubled by recent events, and I suspect you might be brooding over their meaning. I of course feel the meaning of life is best seen out of the corner of the eye—"tell all the truth but tell it slant," as Emily Dickinson once wrote. So instead of bloviating (a good word, it means to go on and on), I will send you what I can, the end of a poem by Matthew Arnold. I think it will appeal to you, acknowledging, as you so often do, the lack of meaning in the world, and yet making a plea that we can still do something about it:

Ah, love, let us be true
To one another! for the world, which seems
To lie before us like a land of dreams,
So various, so beautiful, so new,
Hath really neither joy, nor love, nor light,
Nor certitude, nor peace, nor help for pain;
And we are here as on a darkling plain
Swept with confused alarms of struggle and flight,
Where ignorant armies clash by night.

Why am I sending you such a depressing poem? you might well ask yourself. Well, I send it to you because this poem tells us that we can—_we must!_—make meaning where there is no meaning. We _can_ do it, too,

Alan, through art and beauty and most especially
love. It is all we have, but I think it will suffice.
Be well.

Your fond teacher,
Eliza Perry

P.S. You know Percy Bysshe Shelley, who wrote that
poem "Ozymandias" I gave you? He was famous for
standing up to bullies, too.

Alan looked at the letter a long time. At last he stood up, folded it carefully, and laid it in the secret part of his desk drawer, closing it carefully.

Thursday was a half day at school for Christmas Eve. Alan didn't bother going; he felt he might as well spend the day staring at his own walls than stare at the pockmarked dropped ceiling of Josiah Quincy Junior High. But there was something he needed to do that day, something Mrs. Perry had explained to him. As the poem said, if there was no certitude, no peace, no help for pain, there was still something. There was still friendship, and Alan used to have that. Besides, he was beginning to get restless.

He washed as best he could around the bandages on his broken ribs, and then, slowly, painfully, he dressed. He put on a dark green sweater he had never worn before, swearing as he battled it on, and then he left the house.

All the way over, he felt sick to his stomach with worry

that they wouldn't let him in. At every step, though, he felt the stirrings of bravery in his heart. It *was* a brave thing he was doing, going there even as he worried they would reject him: the old Alan never would have done it.

It was Agnes who answered the door. "Oh," she said bluntly. "It's you."

"Yeah," said Alan. "It's me, and I'm a jerk, and I want you to forgive me."

She started myopically at his black eyes and then asked, irrelevantly, "Why are you wearing that sweater?"

"You guys gave it to me," he answered.

"But you said sweaters were lame."

"So?"

"You said you only wore black."

"Jesus, Agnes! Can't I wear it because you gave it to me and I was a prick about it before and I'm sorry?"

"Well," she said. "I guess you can." And then: "Do you want to come in?"

"*Yes*," he said, rolling his eyes—and then he stopped and started over. "Yes," he amended. "I really do."

Alice stood up in surprise when Alan walked into the kitchen, but then she sat down again and turned away from him.

"Al—" he started. "Hey, Alice, listen—I know there's no reason you should forgive me or anything, and maybe you won't, but I had to come here and tell you this. I don't know how I screwed up so much, and I don't know how I could have believed all that crap about CRAP and maybe I was just crazy and I don't even know what I'm saying now except I want to say I'm sorry and I don't know how."

She turned towards him then, and it was indescribably painful to see how thoroughly he had killed their friendship. He winced. He had never had a better friend than her, and now she hated him.

"You really hurt me," she told him. "You really hurt me, and you're such a jerk I bet you don't even know it."

They were true, her words, and they hurt him to the core. It was all he could do to stand there and take it.

"That's the thing about you, Alan," she went on. "You think you're all smart and perceptive, but you really don't see what's happening around you."

There was nothing to say. She was right. He thought about Juliet, all puffy-eyed, when she'd come to tell him about breaking up with Connor Bumpass. Those were all clues, too, and he hadn't bothered with them at all.

She went on. "Just because you don't have feelings doesn't mean that other people don't. I—"

"Who says I don't have feelings?"

"*You* always do!"

"Well, we've already established that I'm an idiot, haven't we, so why the hell would you trust anything I say?"

They stood there, staring at each other, and then Alice said in a quiet voice, "I can think of *one* reason to forgive you."

"What?"

"I missed you. Come on in. My parents have been making bets for weeks you'd come back on Christmas Eve."

She led him into the bright den, and to Alan's eye each of the candles there seemed surrounded by a halo of light. Then Mr. Parker jumped up from the couch where he had been sitting with his wife and raced over to pump Alan's hand up and down.

"See!" he cried triumphantly after he'd exclaimed over Alan's battered state. "I *told* you he'd be back for the log!" He swept his hand towards the table, and Alan saw it there, the cake shaped like a Yule log with the mossy bits and the little mushrooms made out of marzipan. They always had it on Christmas Eve, and he had always shared it with them. Alan felt a little stunned. Here it was, another Christmas Eve at the Parkers', with the eggnog and the exploding Christmas crackers and the Yule log, and the candles and the expectant tree. Everything had changed and nothing had changed.

"I didn't come back for the log," Alan explained, blushing. He felt he had to confess it, both to tell them he hadn't been that considerate, and to tell them it was *them* he wanted to see, not the marzipan mushrooms. "Really, I forgot all about it. It's just a coincidence I came today." He paused. "Coincidences happen, you know."

"Well, let's toast to coincidences, then," Mrs. Parker said, raising her glass of eggnog. She had a paper crown from the cracker arranged tipsily on her head, and she looked very happy. Alice and Agnes looked happy, too, trimming the tree like they did every Christmas Eve.

He helped them hang the familiar ornaments, the old ones, the ugly ones, the ones they had made with Alan out of spray-painted macaroni back when they were little. Then they pressed him to drink eggnog and eat chestnuts and the traditional first piece of the Yule log cake, and Mrs. Parker kissed him again and welcomed him back.

"So, the prodigal son returns," Mr. Parker said, toasting Alan with his eggnog. And when they asked him what that meant, he told them the parable about the man with the two sons, the wayward one, who went out and gambled and smoked and drank and cavorted with harlots and forgot all about his father, and the other one, who played everything by the book. And then the gambling son, the wasteful son, came slinking back, and the father welcomed him, killing the fattened calf and throwing a big party for him. But the other son—that poor, respectable schmuck of a son—he got nothing.

"Well, that's not fair!" said Alice indignantly, but Alan sort of thought it was. It was another kind of fairness, maybe—because the prodigal son needed it more.

"Can we be okay again?" he asked Alice when he was leaving, standing under the mistletoe on their threshold.

"Is that what you want?" she asked cautiously.

"Of course that's what I want," he said, and he punched her shyly in the arm.

"The sweater matches your black eyes," she said by way of an answer, and she kissed him softly on the cheek.

THE LAST THING THE PRODIGAL SON expected to see when he came home was Juliet waiting in his other room, but there she was.

He didn't want to see her—or rather, he didn't want her to see him. He thought back to the last time she had seen him, bloviating about being involved with mankind and swimming in his own stupid blood, and felt that he would never feel fully dressed in front of her again. He could not meet her eyes.

"Hey," she said shyly. "I kinda rooted through your things while I was waiting—I watched this movie, I hope it's okay. . . ."

He looked at the screen. It was the strange footage he had shot the morning he had planned the stakeout, of the shadows that looked like a bobbing army. He had found it very beautiful then, and now it just made him feel even more naked than ever.

"It's nothing," he said quickly. "Just some things I saw. I don't think it's art, or anything."

"I think it's really beautiful," she said. "It's people, isn't it? You saw people in the grass."

Maybe she understood—shyly, he came into the room and sat next to her.

"I like how you can see things in things," she said, eyes still on the television. "I like that about you. Sometimes I think that's what I admire most about you."

The tape ended. Now he was staring at a blank screen, but it was better than looking at her.

"Charles . . ." she said suddenly. "Listen, Charles, I'm sorry. . . ."

"*You're* sorry?" he said to her stupidly. "Why should *you* be sorry?"

"Because I should have listened to you when you were worried about the governor."

Salt to the wound; he flinched. Maybe she *had* come here to make fun of him, after all. But he deserved it, and this new model of Alan would take it like a man.

"That was all stupid," he told her. "I know I was being crazy."

"But you *cared*," she said. "You really cared about her, and as your friend, I should have cared, too."

He stared at her—this was not at all what he had expected.

"And maybe you weren't *all* that crazy, anyway," she went on. "I mean, I've been thinking about it, and maybe they were up to *something*, you know?"

"What do you mean?" His eyes flew up to hers; maybe she wasn't making fun of him after all.

"I mean, just because they weren't planning an assassination doesn't mean they weren't *criminals*. Lenny *is* a gun dealer, isn't he?"

"Yeah. . . ."

"And we really did hear the Boss threatening him, didn't we?"

"Yeah—we did."

"And remember when I heard them laughing about the dog license, like they were really talking about something else? Maybe they were—maybe they were talking about a different kind of license. . . ."

"You mean a gun license?"

"That's just what I mean, Agent 666."

"You're good, Agent 4X35," he told her in admiration. It was true. "But what?"

"I don't know what. And probably we'll never know what."

"I *need* to know what . . ." he started, but she shrugged.

"Maybe you need to know," she said, answering him as God had answered Job, "but that doesn't mean you *get* to know."

He stole a glance at her again, and saw that she was still looking at him patiently. She sat very close to him, or maybe it was that he was so sensitive to her he could feel her no matter how far away she was. Now he sat there, resting his sore eyes, feeling the fuzz of her sweater just brush against his arm. He felt, at that moment, that he could trust her.

"But somebody still did try to kill the governor," he said, as if it were a confession. "He's still out there—they never caught him."

She nodded.

"I still feel responsible," he said. "Isn't that crazy?"

"I think it's kind of nice," she said quietly.

"I feel responsible for that stupid Kaufman, too," he burst out. "It just sucks! Nothing's going to change for him."

"Well, Rory's been expelled. And he's going to have a hearing or something," she said. "That's something, isn't it?"

"You think it's really going to make a difference to Kaufman?"

"Yes." She paused. "And maybe it makes even more of a difference that you defended him."

Alan snorted. "Some defense," he said, motioning to his ribs.

"It was," she said, very softly.

He looked up at her then; the look on her face wasn't pity. She didn't despise him for coming to Kaufman's aid so pathetically. For a moment, neither of them said anything. Then Juliet started over.

"I don't have ballet class next week," she told him.

"You don't?"

"Not until after New Year's. So I was thinking, maybe we should hang out."

"Hang out?"

"Yeah, *hang out*. You know, play games or something . . . or you know what I'd really like?"

"What?" He felt he could barely talk now—his voice had gone all funny.

"Let's make a movie. Let's go around and you can show me how you see those things you see, and we'll make a movie. Not a *film* or anything," she assured him. "Just a movie. I'd really like that."

"I'd like that, too," he choked. It was true.

There was another pause, and then she said: "Charles?"

There was something in her tone that made the lump in his throat swell. Her side brushed his, and it was electric. He closed his eyes.

"You know—" she started, and stopped awkwardly. "You know, Charles, I still think it would be a big mistake if we went out."

His heart imploded, collapsed. It was as if time had stopped for the moment of his death. In a second she was going to say the words that would nail his coffin shut, but for the moment he could still breathe in the smell of her sweater and feel her body so close to his own. She did not despise him; she wanted to make a movie with him; that would have to be enough.

"I—" She pulled back suddenly, so that he fell heavily against her. He had not realized how much she'd been supporting his weight, and he blushed deeply. They looked at each other with a kind of painful awkwardness now, breathing heavily, but neither looked away.

"Oh, crud," she said, and then she lunged forward and grabbed him. She kissed him hard, on the mouth, and when she pulled back, her eyes were full of tears.

"There it is," she said sadly. "The beginning of the end of our friendship."

But Alan hardly heard her. The cherubs were back, playing their long gold trumpets, and the joyous sound of them was in his ears: *alleluia, alleluia, alleluia.*